by

EVELYN CULBER

CHIMERA

Lucy first published in 2001 by
Chimera Publishing Ltd
PO Box 152
Waterlooville
Hants
PO8 9FS

Printed and bound in Great Britain by
Omnia Books Ltd, Glasgow

LUCY

Evelyn Culber

This novel is fiction – in real life practice safe sex

Chapter One

I can't claim that my conversion to the heady pleasures of CP was as dramatic as the one experienced by St Paul on the road to Damascus or wherever it was, but it was still pretty mind-blowing. It also took much longer for me to embrace the connection between pain and pleasure than it did him to change his ways – but I got there in the end.

It all happened about a year after I had started working for the Lenderby Partnership, a small but increasingly successful advertising agency in London. I had begun as a junior art director and, at the time that my bottom first felt the sting of a punishing hand, had proved myself to the extent that I had just been given my own accounts to work on.

I was earning an excellent salary for a girl recently out of art college, was enjoying the work, getting on well with my colleagues, especially the other half of my all girl team, Chrissie, the copy writer. She was – and is – enviably slim, brunette, quiet, very pretty and good at her job.

So, everything in the garden was lovely. Until I was summoned to see Jonquil Lenderby one Friday afternoon.

I can't claim that I had the slightest premonition that my life was on the verge of radical change as I trotted along to her office. I was still basking in the glow of all the praise that had been lavished on Chrissie and me for our contribution to winning a big new account, and was reasonably confident that Jonquil wanted to add her appreciation.

Not that her opinion was as important as her husband's. He, Clive, had founded the agency five years previously, and she had been his secretary before he took the plunge. Quite rightly appreciating her efficiency, he made her his partner in the new enterprise, then married her and, as far as I knew, it was all working out fine. They seemed able to separate business and leisure without any problems, and she certainly played a vital role in keeping the boring but crucial administrative side of things ticking over smoothly. And her stunning beauty and natural charm were of no hindrance at all when it came to keeping clients happy.

But she never claimed to have an instinctive grasp of what makes good advertising, which is why I wasn't expecting a serious and helpful discussion on the thought processes that had led Chrissie and I to hit on the winning creative approach. On the other hand, I liked her a lot and was just as keen as anyone to stay in her good books. The only barrier between us was that I secretly fancied her husband and often felt pangs of jealously when I spotted those little signs of intimate harmony between them.

I was too wrapped up in my happy mood to notice the coolness of her reception when she asked me to take a seat in her neat office, so what happened next not only had me gawping at her like an idiot, but scattered my wits to such an extent that I was incapable of arguing my case.

It turned out that I had made a cock-up with my expenses for the previous month and, from her point of view, the conclusion that I was on the fiddle was almost unmistakable.

'As you've never done anything like this before, Lucy,' she said coldly, 'I am prepared to give you the benefit of the doubt.'

'Thank you,' I stuttered, desperately trying to pull myself together and explain that it had been inefficiency rather than a criminal nature.

'So I am not going to sack you.'

My mouth opened and closed like a goldfish as I began to realise that it was actually quite serious.

'You're good at your job, Lucy, and I do appreciate that things like expenses and other boring admin chores can be a distraction, but then neither should the accounts people have to waste their time sorting out your inadequacies. That's quite fair, isn't it?'

'Yes, of course,' I stuttered, feeling my cheeks burn as I blushed, mainly due to anger with myself for my carelessness, which had directly led to this embarrassing situation and was ruining what had been a perfect day.

Then she took the wind from my sails. 'As I see it, Lucy, there are two alternatives. Either I note it on your records, where it'll stay for as long as you're with us – and which could well influence your reference – or I punish you myself and nobody will know.'

'Oh… I'll take your punishment, Jonquil,' I replied without thinking to ask for details.

'Excellent,' she said warmly, and I began to relax a

bit until I saw a rather threatening glint in her eye.

I felt as though some unseen hand was squeezing my insides. It was not a nice feeling and what made it worse was that I could not understand it. There was just something about her whole attitude, which suggested that I was in for a nasty surprise. For once, I waited for her to enlarge. I have the fiery temper that usually goes with red hair and my normal reaction when threatened is to go in with all guns blazing, with the normal result that I live to regret the outburst. Thank God, on that occasion reason conquered instinct.

Admittedly, when the echoes of her next sentence eventually faded away, I wished I had made some sort of protest and stopped her in her tracks.

'I am going to smack your bare bottom,' she announced, as though it was the most natural thing in the world.

'Oh!' I exclaimed feebly as I stared at her, hoping I'd misheard but knowing I hadn't.

'Second thoughts, Lucy?' she asked, with the suspicion of a smile.

I gratefully seized the opportunity to consider, and was on the verge of backing out and accepting a black mark on my record, but when I stole another glance at her I felt the first stirrings of strange feelings.

Apart from her beauty, I had often sensed a peculiar empathy between us, even though we had not come into contact that often. She was sitting more or less opposite me, her legs crossed, looking neat and remarkably unflustered, and I was suddenly aware of a sense of inferiority to her. In common with most members of the Creative Department, I claimed that the agency's success depended almost totally on our contribution, with all the others there to support us. At that moment it struck me fairly forcibly that, even though we created the advertising, the Jonquils of this world have a vitally important role. And, for the first time, I sensed the calm, controlled power that had obviously captivated the dishy Clive.

It would not do me any harm to be taken down a peg or two, I admitted to myself.

But by being spanked? As far as I knew I had never been punished that way, even as a kid. Corporal punishment was all part of the bad old days; Charles Dickens etc. I knew it had only just died out in boys' public schools, but then they had been living in the past for far too long anyway. This was the end of the twentieth century. The new millennium wasn't that far off.

On the other hand, even then I was a bit of a bottom girl and had enjoyed a couple of mild affairs with other girls, so the thought of the inevitably intimate contact with a member of my own sex didn't make me want to throw up. My last boyfriend had seemed to get quite a bit of pleasure from my behind. Finally, I remembered using a phone box in the West End and reading some of the cards stuck to the walls, all offering amazing sexual services. As I had made my call, I focused on one from a girl suggesting that naughty boys and girls should contact her for a good spanking, and my giggles at the thought had made the conversation rather disjointed.

All in all, not exactly enough to suggest that I had spent my relatively few years of maturity looking for someone to spank me, but clearly enough to stop me from telling her where to get off.

Jonquil watched me, still smiling slightly but not showing any signs of impatience. Quite suddenly, any resistance faded.

I felt ashamed of my inefficiency and some deep instinct told me that if I submitted, somehow I would rise in her estimation, which was important, both personally and professionally.

'I'll accept the spanking,' I said quietly, looking down at the floor and feeling my cheeks burn as I blushed.

Typically, as soon as I'd committed myself, second thoughts rushed into my seething brain, but I sensed that to try and re-open negotiations would only make things worse. I took several deep breaths in an attempt to steady my nerves – with no noticeable effect.

'Good girl,' she said briskly, and stood up. We'd better use the recording studio, so can you check with Rosie to see whether it's free at… let's see, half past five.'

'Yes, Jonquil,' I whispered, and tottered out.

The studio was free and I spent the next twenty minutes in the ladies, knowing full well that I would not be in any condition to engage in casual conversation with any of my colleagues without making it quite clear that all was not well in my usually happy little world.

With a couple of minutes to go, I quickly washed my damp hands, grabbed a drink of water for my horribly dry throat and slipped into the studio.

The fact that I had not even wondered why she should choose that particular room showed what a state I was in. However, as soon as I sat down at the main console and pretended to be setting up a tape, I worked out that although it was uncomfortably cramped, it had the enormous advantage of being soundproof. The realisation that a bare bottom being smacked must be noisy led me to the conclusion that a smack loud enough to be heard through the solid walls of Jonquil's office would be painful.

I stood up, half longing for her to come and get it over with and half wishing that she would remember an urgent appointment – preferably in Scotland – and so the evil deed would be put off for another day. I paced around in a tight circle, my hands on my threatened bottom, feeling very scared. Even waiting to go into the dentist wasn't nearly as bad. I was just assessing the inspired thought that I could claim to have completely forgotten a dental appointment when the thick door hissed open and Jonquil glided in.

We faced each other for a moment. My legs and hands were trembling, my heart seemed to rise into my throat and its beat thudded in my head.

'Let's get straight on with it, Lucy,' she said, her voice warm. Reassuringly so, and my nerves settled a bit. I watched her shift one of the chairs to the side, move another into the limited space in the middle of the room and sit down.

She reached out and took my hand, gently pulling me forward until I was standing between her parted knees. Her hand felt soft and warm, which reassured me even more.

'I'll take your trousers down first,' she announced evenly, reaching for the button, 'as it's much easier than

11

when you're across my knee.'

It seemed sensible to be compliant, so I held my jumper up. She looked up quickly and gave me another little smile and I felt even better. Until, that is, it struck me that she obviously knew exactly what she was doing. Therefore she had done this before. In which case, it was a reasonable assumption that her hand would make up in experience what it lacked in size and hardness.

I gulped and blushed as she tugged my tight trousers down to my knees, suddenly terribly embarrassed at the thought of her eyes horribly close to my naked thighs and, even worse, the triangular bulge of my sex. I held my breath and hoped like hell that she wouldn't pull my knickers down there and then, so she could see it in all its glory. Just in case, I let go of my jumper and restored at least some of my modesty. My feeling of relief when she let my slacks go and began to guide me round to her right was intense, if short-lived.

As I bent clumsily over her lap, the tightening of my knickers over my up-thrust bottom acted as a sharp reminder of what lay in store for me, and my heartbeat accelerated. Acting purely on instinct, I shuffled around until I was fairly comfortable, with my weight evenly distributed between hands, feet and middle, and then lay there, holding my breath, waiting meekly for the supreme indignity of having my knickers pulled down.

Understandably, my thoughts were racing.

I can remember being surprised at how soft her thighs were. I had vaguely envied Jonquil's slim figure, although I had never looked that closely – and she never wore anything figure-hugging, so I had never had much to go on.

The temptation to ask her if I could be spanked over my knickers flitted briefly through my mind, and I was just trying to think of a convincing reason when I felt her fingers delving in the waistband, and knew I was too late.

She bared me quite quickly, and when I felt cool air on my skin my insides seemed to shrivel up and I slumped helplessly on her lap, just failing to prevent the escape of a pathetic little whimper.

The next minute dragged on and on and seemed more like an hour. She put one hand on the small of my back, the other on my left thigh, just below the buttock – and waited. I could just hear her breathing and knew with awful certainty that she was studying my bare bottom.

It is difficult to describe how I felt. My behind felt horribly naked and vulnerable, which didn't surprise me in the least. As I had never been spanked I had no preconception about the amount of pain involved, and so was not too worried about this aspect. Her hand felt small and soft and therefore not especially threatening.

Neither did I feel particularly stupid, in spite of my position. I didn't know it at the time, but there is definitely a submissive streak in me, so lying there across another woman's lap with my bottom deliberately bared, wasn't the same massive outrage to my dignity it would have been to the majority of girls of my generation.

I suppose that deep down I was getting a bit of a kick from the fact that the lovely Jonquil was focusing her full attention on my bottom.

Then she began to spank me and my complacency

about the pain was shattered almost at once. I could not believe how much it stung and I very nearly wriggled off her lap after the first six or so. I think it was pride which kept me in position more than anything else – once I had admitted to myself that I deserved to be punished and had accepted that having my bare bottom smacked was the lesser of the two evils she'd offered me, I felt a growing determination to show her that I could take it reasonably well.

I gritted my teeth, tightened as many muscles as was necessary to keep me in position and concentrated fully on the reason for my spanking. As her hand danced rhythmically over the full surface of my bottom, I kept reminding myself that I had been silly and careless and deserved everything I was getting.

Not that it worked all the way through. As Jonquil made my poor bottom hotter and hotter, the sound of her hand hitting me filled my seething brain and that maddening, stinging pain dominated me to the exclusion of everything else. I began to buck and heave on her lap, despite the increasing pressure of her left hand on the small of my back.

I could no longer stop myself crying out and begging her to stop.

She spoke for the first time since she'd put me across her knee. 'Stop being silly, Lucy. Your bottom's still only pink and I'm not stopping until it's nice and red. All over. Now keep still, girl! Otherwise I'll smack your legs,' she added and, to make the threat absolutely clear, spanked me sharply three times on the top of each thigh.

The pain was very different to what I'd felt before,

even though the skin there was unmarked. I cried out and had to dig my toes hard into the carpet to stop myself kicking.

'Well, Lucy,' she asked as the echo of the sixth still rang in my ears, 'legs or bottom?'

'Oh, definitely my bottom, please Jonquil,' I said fervently.

'Fine. But keep it still, then.'

'Yes, Jonquil.'

In some strange way, actually asking her to smack me on my bottom made a difference. I was able to appreciate that there was a markedly different quality to the pain in the traditional area. Much later, I learnt that this is largely due to the fact that a smack on the bottom sends ripples into a girl's anus and vagina, which she may not feel at the time but still adds something to the sensation. As it was, I could only be grateful for small mercies and lie there taking it as well as I could.

I was just beginning to feel an underlying warmth spreading through my middle when she stopped and began to stroke my burning cheeks with surprising – and very welcome – tenderness. My eyes began to fill with tears as I realised my punishment was over, and I no longer had to keep fighting my own weakness.

Her hand was lovely and soothing and I lay there panting and rapidly coming to the conclusion that being spanked on the bare bottom was a very effective punishment! The pain was beginning to die away, and Jonquil's comforting hand was doing a hell of a lot more than simply soothe the burning. Somehow she was letting me know that as far as she was concerned, all was forgiven and the slate was wiped clean.

I was just telling myself to make absolutely sure that I never did anything which would lead to a repeat dose, when she gave my bottom a couple of little slaps.

'You took that really well, considering it was your first time, Lucy… I am right, you've never had your bottom smacked before, have you?'

'No, I haven't,' I admitted.

'I thought not. Well done.'

'Thank you,' I replied, absurdly pleased.

'And you've got a lovely bottom, by the way,' she added dreamily, trailing her fingertips down the cleft between my hot cheeks.

'Oh!' I exclaimed, genuinely surprised. I may have had a bit of a thing about the human rear, but I had never thought of mine as especially attractive; a little bit on the big side, in my opinion at least, and only one boyfriend had really paid any attention to it. I enjoyed that and, as he was a considerate guy, I was doubly sorry when he went abroad. I had never got as far as bottoms with the few girls I'd flirted with, so Jonquil's obviously genuine praise not only took me aback but also made her intimate caresses even nicer.

All too soon another couple of slaps signalled the end of the session, and an hour later I was back home, for once angry that there was nobody around and I was alone with my thoughts. I had a long shower, during which the conflicting impressions of the pain and indignity of being spanked and the gentle attention afterwards battled for domination. I snatched a quick supper and then decided that I would go mad if I stayed at home

16

alone with my uncertainties, so changed and drifted down to the local pub, where I greeted a crowd of acquaintances with relief.

It turned out to be a rather boozy and very happy weekend, and I struggled to the office on Monday with a slight hangover and my inner conflict temporarily forgotten.

It came back into my mind the following evening. My flatmates were all out, and after a shower I found myself taking a long hard look at my naked reflection in a full length mirror, appraising not just my body but seeing if having no clothes on would give me some insight into the aspect of my personality Jonquil seemed to have brought to the surface.

I had never considered myself a beauty. Not that I'd ever lost much sleep over my looks because I received enough flattering attention to feel attractive, and in my few self-analytical moods, I had actually been grateful for my lack of potential as a model or whatever, as I had learnt from the less than happy experiences of a gorgeous girl at secondary school that outstanding looks can be as much of a burden as a blessing.

My hair was okay; auburn rather than red, and my complexion matched my general colouring; pale, clear but with a slightly freckled face.

My figure looked reasonable, although I suspected that the mirror may have flattered me a little. My boobs are big enough to fill a lover's hand, with some left over, my nipples are a pale pink and quite small but pucker nicely when properly handled, and my waist is narrow. My legs are nice and long but not as slender as I would have wanted at that time, although I'm happier with them now.

Turning round, I peered back to look at my bottom, studying it carefully for the first time in years, and seeing it with a different perspective after all the attention Jonquil had given it. I still felt it was too big, but had to admit that it was rather nicely curved, with full cheeks, a tight crack down the middle and rather eye-catching folds where cheeks and thighs met. I gave it a few experimental pats, and did find both the visual and tactile signs of softness appealing, and began to understand Jonquil just a bit better.

Satisfied that I didn't have that much to worry about, and deciding that I needn't go on a crash diet, I began to think more about the mental effects of my spanking, getting dressed again and moving to the sitting room with a cup of coffee, always a useful aid to mental effort. The most vivid memory at the time was the feeling of well-being after I'd cooled down. My bottom had glowed in a way that was almost sexy, but it was my mind that had reacted most strongly. I soon worked out that easily the most important factor in my submission was Jonquil. My basic respect for her beauty and capabilities had been clouded by my silly jealousy, but the memory of those incredible blue eyes challenging me to resist her punishment and her enigmatic smile when I caved in made me squirm with a combination of shame and confusion. And yet, it never occurred to me to regret my actions – apart of course, from the stupidity of trying to pull the wool over her eyes in the first place.

To my relief Jonquil treated me with noticeably more

respect than before, and in a couple of days my spanking seemed no more than a bad dream. I was vaguely aware that I was sharper and more incisive at work, but put that down to biorhythms, and simply enjoyed the feeling that my efforts were increasingly valued by one and all.

I was especially pleased that Chrissie and I were really knitting together as a team. She never seemed to mind when I made some tentative suggestions on a thorny problem with copy, and her ideas on the visual side of our projects were always worth listening to.

I began to look at Jonquil more often and more closely. Her immaculate appearance and calm progress through each working day were quite enough to annoy a scruff like me, but somehow I felt increasingly in awe of her. I found myself actually envying Clive rather than her when I saw them together, remembering the feel of her thighs under my tummy, the knowledge that her gaze was fixed on my naked bottom, and the varied sensations from her hands on my flesh.

But for all that, I had no desire to spend another minute gazing at the carpet in the studio, being far more anxious to stay in her good books.

About six weeks after my spanking I was supervising the shooting of a TV commercial for one of our lesser clients, a cosmetics company who was launching a new line in shower gels. We had tried hard to come up with a completely original idea but without success, so had settled on the obvious, i.e. an attractive young professional woman as the main character, with the first ten seconds showing flashes of her at her desk, stuck in heavy traffic, etc, all illustrating a pretty horrendous day.

Then she gets home and immediately starts undressing, ending up with her in the bathroom and in the shower. The last ten seconds were of her visibly relaxing beneath the water, and the final shot was a still of her holding the bottle and inhaling deeply, a happy smile on her face. Cue to pack shot.

In the end the campaign worked well, with sales over what had been generally considered an optimistic forecast. I cheerfully accepted some of the credit, although freely admitting that the director had excelled himself. Having discovered a small talent for photography at art college, I loved being in on the shoots for our ads and, of course, as art director, it was very much part of my job.

I let the production team get on with the hectic day sequences and duly turned up for the shower scene. All was going fine, the model was on time for once and we were all set for the first shot – of her coming into her house and stripping off. I had planned it so that the camera would basically follow her feet, picking the trail of discarded clothing on the way. To save the girl's blushes, the idea was that she would wear two sets of undies, so we would see her bra and knickers falling to the floor but she wouldn't have to worry about being naked when it wasn't strictly necessary.

But to my amazement she spurned my offer. 'You're all going to see everything I've got when we do the shower bit, so what the hell,' she said.

It took quite a few takes before the director and I were both satisfied, especially of the last few feet, when she dropped her bra and panties. At first I was a bit bemused, because from what I could see we could have wrapped up that bit after the second attempt. Then I noticed that the camera was definitely pointing above Sharon's legs – at her bare bottom. My first reaction was annoyance at such a typically male trick, but before I could say anything I actually watched her twitching little rump for the first time and suddenly realised how attractive a girl's bottom can be, especially when she's walking.

After a while I sneaked behind the cameraman and whispered in his ear. 'If you don't let me have a tape of that bit, I'll tell on you.' His answering grin was suitably embarrassed and he agreed without any protest.

Otherwise, the shoot went well and I was confident that we would achieve the desired result. Then two more highly significant things happened. When we called it a day a dripping Sharon emerged from the shower, winked at me and then bent down to pick up her towel. By then the crew had moved off in search of tea, so we were alone and this encouraged me to give her tight bare bottom a juicy smack. She straightened up with a squeal and immediately started to rub the afflicted cheek, while I stammered an apology on the lines that I had never been able to resist an attractive bottom. Totally untrue, but it was the best excuse I could come up with on the spur of the moment.

And to my huge relief she just grinned at me. Then she put on a pained expression. 'You're rotten, Lucy, you really are,' she whined, as she craned over her shoulder at the injured bit. 'Look, you caught me on this side, not across the middle, and I'm all uneven.'

I am quite sure that if it hadn't been for Jonquil I would have done no more than to offer to rub the red patch better – if that. As it was, the memory of the yielding flesh under my palm was lingering rather nicely, and I was curious to see things from Jonquil's point of view.

'I'd better even you up then,' I announced firmly, and tucked her under my left arm.

'Oh, you wicked, cruel bitch,' she wailed, and for a second I wondered if I had already overstepped the mark, but then she stuck her pretty bottom out a bit further and any doubts flew out of the window. I bent forward so that I had an even better view, rubbed the bright pink mark speculatively, and then transferred my attention to the other side, resting my hand on the target area and pressing to test the resilience. Until that moment I hadn't fully appreciated how soft a girl's bottom can be. Sharon's was neat and quite firm, but the way my hand sank in came as something of a surprise – and a very pleasant one, too. I could easily have spent several minutes exploring, but I knew that the crew would be back soon, so I let fly and connected beautifully.

Sharon squealed, her whole bottom quivered deliciously and she tried to straighten up, but I held her firmly, telling her that I wanted to make sure I'd hit the right spot. She sighed theatrically, but stayed bent as I watched the pink patch develop, and then I told her that both cheeks were pretty evenly matched. I gave her a couple of pats for good measure and let her go. She trotted off to find her clothes, wiggling her bottom saucily as she went and turning to stick her tongue out at me just as

22

she disappeared.

In an excellent mood, I started clearing up.

That day proved the old saying that good things come in threes. I had enjoyed a prolonged view of a female bottom, had smacked it, and would have been quite content if that had been all the day offered in rude pleasures.

An hour later everything was clear and tidy, the director and most of the crew had left, leaving me to wait for the owners of the house we'd rented for the day, show them that we left it as we found it and pay them.

Greg the cameraman offered to stay and keep me company, and I accepted his offer with alacrity. He was nice looking, quiet and self-effacing. I particularly liked his shy smile and the way he seemed able to sit quietly for hours, gazing dreamily into the distance, his mind clearly lingering on lighting, focus, framing and angles. We had worked together on several films and we chatted easily about various technicalities. Then he unexpectedly broke one of the pauses in the conversation.

'Do you still want a tape of the walking bit?' he asked.

'Yes, of course,' I replied, rather too eagerly, for he gave me a sideways look. I was just about to make some lame excuse for my interest when I decided that it was none of his business anyway, and just grinned at him.

'Okay, I'll spice it up a bit and send it over to the agency.'

'Fine.'

'Did you like her bum?'

I hesitated for a second or two, trying to give the

impression that I hadn't really thought about it. 'Yes, quite pert,' I eventually said. 'What about you?'

'Too small for my taste,' he replied rather dismissively. 'I much prefer yours.'

As I had imagined that her typical model's figure was right up his street, I was surprised as well as flattered. 'How do you know?' I laughed. 'You haven't seen it.'

And he looked me straight in the eye. 'I'd like to,' he said. 'Can I?'

The events of the day had wound me up nicely and the thought of him gazing appreciatively at my bare bottom was tempting. 'All right,' I said quietly, and stood up with my back to him, quickly undid the top button of my jeans, pulled the zip down and waited passively, my arms at my sides.

To my relief Greg showed a rare sensitivity for a man. Rather than rip my jeans and knickers down, he eased them southwards one at a time, nice and slowly with plenty of pauses, presumably to have a good look at the flesh he had just uncovered. When my knickers were clear of my bottom I heard a deep sigh and felt really pleased at the subtle compliment – and even better when he started to fondle my bare buttocks with a gentle and expert touch.

It really was terrific. In something of a daze I found myself on all fours with my naked rear in the air and with Greg playing me with all the skill of a top musician with his favourite instrument. Apart from Jonquil, nobody had ever devoted so much time and care to my bottom, and I loved every second of it. With one hand stroking and squeezing my taut cheeks, he trailed the fingertips

24

of the other up and down my cleft, and in no time at all I was crouching right down and pushing my hips as far into the air as I could, openly offering myself to him.

He made me come quite quickly and I stayed in position trying to get my breath back. Then I felt something smooth and hard nuzzle against my bottom-hole and begin to press against the tight little ring. I was so spaced out that it took several seconds before I cottoned on to the fact that I was on the verge of losing my second virginity! My natural instinct was to hunch my hips inwards, trapping his cock in the fleshy embrace of my decently closed cleft.

'Er, Greg,' I whispered cautiously, very conscious of my vulnerability. 'I don't think you should be doing that…'

'Haven't you had it up your bottom before?' he grunted.

'No, I haven't,' I insisted. 'And I'm not sure that I want to now.'

'You haven't lived,' he said.

There was a pregnant pause, and I honestly think that if I hadn't been spanked I would have gotten away from him, but the clear memories of the strangely exciting sensations I'd felt from my sore bottom had obviously changed my perceptions and the thought of his cock in the tightness of my back passage suddenly tempted me.

'All right,' I panted against my forearm, and waited anxiously.

My feelings were very much the same as when Jonquil had put me across her knee. My bottom was bare and prominently displayed, I was facing the prospect of unknown discomfort, or even pain, and my position was overtly submissive. The normal part of me wanted to revolt against being dominated, but my curiosity was stronger.

I felt my sex get hot and moist again. A tingling ache in my nipples made me cup my breasts and squeeze them through my thin shirt. For some reason, the fear of the unknown had made me even more randy.

Greg put his hands on the cheeks of my bottom and eased them further apart. My breath hissed through my clenched teeth as the stretching of my anus sent little stabs of pain up my back passage, but when he began to open and close my buttocks in a gentle rhythm I started to relax and the pain changed to waves of pleasure. I could feel the tight muscle of my sphincter slowly loosen under his expert ministrations, and my fear gradually receded.

Then I felt something touch my anus and heard faint squelching sounds as I suddenly realised that I was getting all slippery back there. I peered over my shoulder and tucked my bottom in. 'What are you doing?' I demanded.

'KY jelly. Found it in the bathroom.' His voice was strained and I saw his reddened face and bulging eyes staring at my bottom. It was all beginning to get dangerously exciting. With my jeans and knickers down my bottom felt especially naked as I crouched down and, as he gently covered my anus with lubricant, I was tingling nicely. Then he slipped a finger inside me and that really did feel sexy, so I pushed my hips back until I could feel his knuckles press against the inner surfaces

26

of my buttocks and squeezed my sphincter tightly on the intruding digit. I began to pant and moan as the strange sensations spread deeper and deeper, and then he pulled his finger out and I held my breath, listening impatiently to him putting on a condom. I felt something press against my anus and instinctively bore down, and the tight little muscle gave slightly, enough to let him get the tip of his prick past the entrance.

Then, all of a sudden, it was all pain.

I groaned aloud and, if Greg hadn't been gripping me firmly by the hips, I'm sure I would have wriggled free. As it was the stunning shock as he stretched me beyond endurance kept me still long enough for him to penetrate me fully.

'Keep still,' he ordered through gritted teeth, and I just had enough sense to obey.

It was very unpleasant indeed. Physically, my bottom-hole felt as if it was being split, my rectum felt horribly full and his fingers were digging into my hips so hard it hurt. And I suddenly felt a surge of disgust at being poked in the one part of my body that, until then, I had done my best to ignore. But something deep inside stopped me from pulling away. I knew some girls got quite a kick out of being buggered, and so resolved at least to give it a fair chance, reasoning that it could hardly get worse.

And I was right. After a few slow and gentle thrusts, each one a little deeper, Greg was buried to the hilt and I could feel his rather hairy tummy pressed up against the cheeks of my bottom. He then kept still for a moment or two, and the pause was enough to let me get my breath back. I felt the tension drain away as my anus began to get used to the invasion and slowly the horrible prickling ache subsided and was replaced with a much nicer sensation.

Then he reached underneath and found his way to my sex lips, probing until he was right on the button and the thrilling waves from that sensitive little spot suddenly made everything fall into place.

My bottom began to move back and forth and I began to enjoy the friction of his prick in the tightness of my rectum. I took deep steady breaths as I tried to concentrate on my throbbing anus and soon found that if I pushed down and then squeezed it tightly around his shaft, it added to my pleasure and, judging from his groans, a lot to Greg's.

Unfortunately, just as I was reaching the conclusion that having a man up one's bottom was actually exciting, Greg came. I crouched there, seething with frustration before it occurred to me to use my own hand to bring myself off, which I did successfully, helped by the strange sensation of his cock getting soft in my bottom.

Unfortunately, a few minutes later we were both recovering when we heard a car outside and realised that the owners of the house had returned, so rather than indulging in a nice post-coital cuddle, we had to make ourselves decent in an undignified rush.

When I lay in bed that night I found that the excitements of the day made sleep impossible, so I decided to put the events of the previous few weeks into perspective.

Since Jonquil had spanked me, bottoms had begun to

play a more prominent role in my life. As I relived the various and varied impressions, I began to realise that there were some very disturbing aspects slowly emerging.

Firstly, from my spanking – admittedly, I'd had good reasons to submit to what still struck me as an old-fashioned and predominantly childish punishment, but I had submitted, and done so with virtually no resistance and the memory still retained an element of bitter self-recrimination.

Then, I had presented my even more nakedly exposed bottom to Greg, meekly allowing him to perform a pretty taboo act on me.

In both instances I had derived some pleasure from the submissive positions, and the thought that there were previously unsuspected depths to my personality was disturbing.

On the other hand, the hour or so I had spent looking at Sharon's bare bottom had certainly aroused my interest in this part of the human anatomy, especially the female. Her trim but mobile cheeks had fascinated me and made both Jonquil's and Greg's interest in my bottom far more understandable.

Being spanked and buggered had been painful. In the former case, that was the whole idea of course, but when Greg penetrated me it had not taken that long for the pain to turn me on, to the extent that I definitely pushed my bottom against him, rather than pull away.

Then I remembered how the stinging had faded to a really nice tingling glow quite soon after Jonquil had stopped spanking me.

Was I a masochist?

If so, was there anything wrong with that?

I had just reached the conclusion that if I were, then there wasn't a great deal I could do about it and, in any case, both Jonquil and Greg were attractive and talented, and both appealed to different desires within me.

And on that note I dropped off to sleep.

Luckily, I was so busy that those disturbing thoughts stayed buried for some time, only surfacing for a short while when Greg sent the tape. He had done an amazing job with it, spinning it out to last about fifteen minutes, repeating the sequence a number of times in increasingly slow motion, so that every little wiggle and sway could be enjoyed at leisure. After I'd watched it for the third time I came to the conclusion that, given the choice, I would rather spank Sharon's bare bottom than have Jonquil smack mine – and felt a lot better about myself.

Three days later, however, and confusion reigned again; I incurred Jonquil's displeasure once more.

Apart from all her other talents, Jonquil had a terrific voice, and so we used her quite often to do voice overs, especially for radio adverts, and I asked her to do the one for the shower gel film. There wasn't much to it; as the camera zoomed in for the statutory pack shot, all Jonquil had to say was, 'Cleans... soothes... and moisturises'. I knew she would only need a couple of takes at most, so having cleared it with her secretary, I booked the recording studio and got on with my work.

I was just getting ready to start setting everything up for her when she slipped into my little office and told me I'd made another cock up with my expenses, and as I started to apologise I saw a predatory glint in her eyes.

Her intentions were perfectly obvious and, frankly, there was no need for her to tell me so pointedly that I was going to get spanked again, on my bare bottom. Especially as my office was anything but soundproof and there were people next door.

I felt my face burn with embarrassment, and the combination of trepidation and resentment induced the sensation of a hand gripping my innards and squeezing. Then my bottom began to tingle and the blood drained from my face as I realised that I was feeling a strange excitement as well.

We went to the studio, and I was in such a state that it took over a dozen takes before we got the timing exactly right, and as I rewound the master tape she made me feel even worse.

'Extra for that display of incompetence, Lucy,' she announced calmly, to which I stammered something about finding it hard to concentrate when I was about to be punished, and she replied with a devastating remark about a lack of professionalism. Then she got down to business.

With a dry mouth and constricted throat I watched Jonquil move her chair clear of the console, sit down and pat her lap. Then, as I approached, our eyes met and I could see quite clearly that she was intensely excited at the prospect of having my bare bottom completely at her mercy; there was a tightness to her mouth and a pink flush coloured her graceful throat, disappearing into her neat blouse.

The incontrovertible proof that spanking me turned her on came as such a surprise that I gasped. We stared at each other for several seconds and, in that short time, I realised that it was probably my last chance to break free of her clutches and revert to the independent young career girl I had been until very recently. But she reached out, took my hand and gently pulled me closer. For a moment I resisted and we remained still, our eyes locked. Hers silently challenged me to accept what she clearly knew to be an essential submissiveness, while I fought a brief battle with my own fears, instinctively knowing that if I meekly accepted the spanking, I would be under her thumb for the foreseeable future.

Suddenly the strength drained from my legs and I collapsed over her lap. I can remember feeling her thighs shift softly beneath me, and her hands on my buttocks guiding me until I'd settled. Then she stroked the tightened seat of my skirt and my bottom tingled beautifully. For a moment or two I wondered if she had changed her mind and was going to spank me over my skirt and, showing how much I had changed, I felt a flare of disappointment at the thought.

Needless to say, I was wrong. She was just reminding herself of the contours and consistency of my cheeks – and, of course, adding to the agony of waiting. Before long she was tugging my skirt slowly upwards and, immediately it was folded on my back, set about pulling first my tights and then my knickers down to my knees.

I held my breath as my bottom was finally bared, and to this day I can still remember the strange thrill I felt as the elastic waistband slithered down over my rounded cheeks and relatively cool air caressed the slowly increasing expanse of naked skin. The fear of imminent pain was considerably reduced by the way Jonquil pulled my knickers down so sensuously.

And what finally made me accept that I got a kick from being spanked, even by another woman, was when she gently patted both bare cheeks and then broke the silence.

'Such a lovely bottom.' She said something similar the first time, but I'd forgotten about it.

'Is… is it really?' I asked nervously.

'Of course,' she confirmed, as her hands roamed freely.

'Oh,' I replied weakly, at a loss for words. 'Thank you,' I added, remembering my manners.

Then she started to spank me.

Whether she did it more lightly than she had the first time, or whether it was because I was distracted by the compliment, I couldn't tell. What I did appreciate was that I actually enjoyed the overture.

She left an interval between each spank, so that I had ample time to feel my bottom quiver and absorb the warm sting before feeling the next one, rather than fight the pain, which had been my main priority the first time.

I soon realised that Jonquil had settled into a rhythmic pattern and, now that I'd begun to come to terms with my submissive side, I was able to appreciate it all far more than before. She started at the base of my buttocks and gave me a smack on each cheek. Then she moved upwards, first on the left side, then the right. By the eighth smack she had reached the top of my bottom and it was tingling all over.

Then she went back down to the lowest part and started all over again, only smacking each side twice in succession.

After that it was three per cheek. Then four and finally five, by which time my bottom was really pretty sore and distinctly warm.

Then she stopped and began to stroke me. For a second I wondered if that was it, and interestingly my first thought was that she was letting me off too lightly. Although I was quite hot and bothered I had already advanced far enough to know that I had not been punished enough, but then sensing it was no more than a temporary cease fire, I relaxed and enjoyed the break, getting my breathing under some sort of control and generally tuning my mind to take the rest as well as I felt I had taken the start.

It therefore took a while before I appreciated that there was something different in the way she was soothing me. The first time she had just stroked my buttocks, but that second session was much more sensual. Once she'd rubbed away the worst of the stinging she began to trail the tips of her fingers all over, lingering first on the little folds at the join of cheeks and legs, and then drifting towards the cleft.

It was fantastic. Especially when she began to delve between my thighs, getting thrillingly close to my most sensitive parts. I pressed down with my feet to lift my bottom and make it all even more accessible to her, and irrepressible moans of pleasure made it quite clear that I was enjoying it.

'Such a lovely bottom,' she cooed, turning me on even more, but then all too soon she decided it was time to resume the punishment. I felt her forearm pressing down on my back and her hand gripped my hip. My heart started fluttering again and I took a series of deep breaths, then her right hand sank into my left buttock as she repeated the same process, steadily building up the pain and the tension.

And the pleasure.

She was smacking me hard enough for the sound to ring loudly in the cramped room and I could feel my rump wobble quite violently every time. Even so, the spreading heat seemed to stimulate more than just my bottom. My sex, which had been tingling deliciously during the stroking, still sent waves into my middle and the noise and the pain of my spanking seemed to mingle in a most amazing way.

Not surprisingly, however, after a few minutes the sexy feelings began to ebb away and the pain started to predominate. I had been trying my utmost to keep my bottom as still as possible, instinctively aware that Jonquil's measured approach to spanking me would be much less effective if she didn't have a steady target to aim at, but I could no longer resist the temptation to snatch it away from the metronomic torment of her tireless palm.

And the results were predictable.

'Keep your bottom still, Lucy!' she snapped, and gave me three on each thigh to remind me that it was worse there than on my buttocks.

'S-sorry, Jonquil,' I panted. 'But it's very sore.' If I

had hoped for sympathy, I was disillusioned.

'That's the main point of a spanking, you silly girl,' she retorted, thankfully restraining herself from emphasising the point with another volley of spanks. 'But you've been very good so far,' she continued, 'so I'll give you a break. Would you like me to rub your bottom again?'

'Oh, yes *please*,' I gasped gratefully.

The second soothing proved even nicer than the first, and I was really turned on by the time she resumed beating me. I had to suffer one more progressive series – from one to five per cheek – and then she tested my newfound resolve to the limit by going back from five to one. It was during this phase that I really grasped the strange and disturbing fact that there was something in my make-up that found excitement in genuine pain in my bare bottom. As she spanked me I distracted myself by recalling images of Sharon, first from Greg's tape and then when I'd smacked her. The pleasure I derived from those two spanks suddenly made Jonquil's fondness for smacking my bottom completely comprehensible, and that thought made me even more determined to submit to her properly.

And then she stopped, and I burst into tears as my bottom really did feel as though it had been stung by a swarm of angry wasps, but her soothing hands soon helped me recover, and I was hoping she'd finished with me when she made me anxiously hold my breath.

'A lovely red bottom,' she said as she moulded a seething cheek in each hand. Not knowing how to respond, I said nothing; just winced as the touching reminded me of how sore I was. Then I stiffened as I felt her fingers dig into the inner curves of my cheeks and begin to ease them apart, opening the valley between them.

Every instinct shrieked at me to clench my buttock muscles as tightly as I could. Greg had parted me before oiling my bottom-hole and I hadn't minded that too much, but to have another female inspecting my anus for no good reason that I could think of was disturbing, to say the least.

But the fact that I managed to resist the desire to tighten up was clear evidence that I really was under her control after just two spankings – plus, of course, her beauty and breeding. So, gritting my teeth and feeling a little sick, I lay there meekly and submitted to having my anus closely inspected.

'Very, very, pretty,' she sighed, and it was the breathless tone of her voice as much as the unexpected compliment that thrilled me.

First Greg and now Jonquil had both examined the one part of my bottom that, until then, I had done my best to ignore and that I definitely thought should only be seen by properly qualified members of the medical profession.

I realised I had an awful lot to learn about sex, and so was in an even more subdued frame of mind when Jonquil decided to give me the extra smacks for my clumsiness with the voice over session, with me crouching on the floor, my bottom thrust as high as I could get it.

There was a small coffee stain on the carpet right in

front of my nose and, by focusing on that and beginning to revel in my deliciously lewd position, I took the extra spanking with hardly a cry, though I could appreciate that her hand stung my taut buttocks even more than before.

When she smacked the very sensitive flesh around my anus my eyes began to water; when she actually delivered a few sharp smacks with the tips of her fingers on my bottom-hole, I nearly came; and when she used her free hand to touch my sex while her spanking hand maintained the rhythmic assault on my poor vulnerable bottom, I did come.

After that day I was a very different person. I was far more aware of more subtle sexual and sensual stimulations, adding a completely new quality to any number of things that until then I had taken for granted. For example, I learnt to enjoy the taste of drink as much as the effect, whether it was the complex taste of a good wine or the sharply refreshing impact of a strong lager when I was really thirsty.

I showed much more interest in food, and even bought some cookery books.

One idle Saturday I revisited the National Gallery and saw the paintings through new eyes, especially the nudes.

I began to use sweet reason rather than aggression with friends and colleagues. One particular example was when we were putting the finishing touches to the shower gel advert and I slowly came to the conclusion that it had to be forty-five seconds rather than the scheduled thirty. This obviously put a considerable extra load on the media department, and the creative director shamelessly admitted that there was no way he was going to break the news to them. So I accused him of craven cowardice, he cheerfully agreed and, with heart in mouth, I made an appointment to see the media director. Whereas before I am sure I would have blustered and made light of the additional hassle, I acknowledged the problem from the outset, showed him both versions of the film and generally played the whole thing straight. He huffed and puffed for a bit, then agreed that the longer version was a lot more effective and agreed to rework the schedule, thanking me for explaining it all properly.

Another lesson learned; that time the easy way.

Watching the tape Greg had sent me made me increasingly keen to spank another girl – properly; not just a couple of quick swats. I really fancied the thought of having some pretty and contrite female totally under my control; to order her across my knee, to bare her bottom and feel my hand sinking into the lovely firm softness of her cheeks, then to stroke her better and assure her that all was forgiven and that I still liked her.

But as the days passed the memory of being across Jonquil's knee began to dominate. I was tempted to make a deliberate cock-up of my expenses, simply to give her the excuse to spank me, and it was only the thought that she may not realise that it was intentional and assume that I was hopelessly inefficient that stopped me.

It didn't occur to me to go and see her, to explain how

she had made me come to terms with my innate – and, until then, unsuspected – submissiveness, and to ask her to smack my bare bottom. Understandably so, really, as I was rather wary of her in those days. Nobody had ever reduced me to a quivering jelly in the way that she had done during my second spanking, and I suppose it was a matter of basic pride which made me shy away from recalling too many of the embarrassing details – except during the occasional sleepless night, when my stubborn mind seemed to force me to remember both the physical and mental sensations and to remind me that I had found them intensely thrilling.

The next stage in my development started when Chrissie and I were on location, and between us we mislaid an expensive camera. As soon as we realised what we'd done I made a frantic taxi trip back to the house, retrieved the camera and, hugely relieved, raced back to the office, confident that all was well.

Wrong! Jonquil, as usual, sensed I'd been up to mischief and the result was that Chrissie and I were summoned to her office. In my innocence, I hoped Chrissie's involvement would spare my bottom from well-deserved retribution, so accepted full responsibility. If I was going to be punished, the last thing I wanted was for Chrissie to know about it. We were already quite close friends but there are some things that should be hidden from even soul mates, and the fact that I was spanked definitely came into that category. I was also conscious of a need to protect my gentle friend.

After I had said my piece, Jonquil frowned thoughtfully. 'I see,' she said, and then her phone rang.

She answered it, asked the caller to hold on, looked up and said she'd get back to us.

'Hopefully she'll have cooled down before she has time to see us,' I said to Chrissie as we went back to our office, 'and we won't get such a big ticking off.'

She smiled at me and then said that she had a meeting with the research department, so slipped away.

An hour later Jonquil came in. 'Another good spanking, Lucy,' she said.

Immediately I felt that horrible hand take a grip of my insides and my heartbeat accelerated. I stood up, ready to accompany her to the studio, fear and excitement building equally.

'Unfortunately,' she continued, 'the studio is fully booked today. But Clive's away until tomorrow, so you'd better come to our flat. Six o'clock all right?'

'Um, yes, fine,' I stammered.

'Good, see you then.'

By the time the taxi drew up to the discreet block of flats in Docklands, I was feeling a lot better and anticipating the thrill more than the pain and shame. I was directed to the lift by the security man, rocketed up eight floors, and found myself in a beautiful lobby with a solid door right ahead. Trying to gather my composure, I rang the bell.

Jonquil greeted me with a warm smile, a hug and a kiss on both cheeks, all of which made me feel calmer, and I followed her into the sitting room. But as I closed the door behind me several things stopped me dead in my tracks. Firstly, the size and the sheer elegance of the room. Secondly, the amazing view of the Thames through the panoramic windows. Thirdly, and most devastating of all, a nervously smiling Chrissie.

I gawped at her. 'You as well!' I cried.

'Yes,' she replied, simply.

My poor beleaguered brain could take no more and I hardly heard Jonquil reminding us of our joint crime and announcing that we were both to be punished. My first reaction was an unworthy flare of jealousy. Presumably I'd hoped that the spankings formed a special bond between Jonquil and me, and learning that mine was not the only bottom she had at her mercy was a blow to my pride.

Then I felt guilty about that and looked searchingly at my friend, hoping to see some sign that she felt the same about being spanked as I did. She was understandably pale and tense, but didn't seem alarmed by it all. That reassured me, and I suddenly realised that I would probably be able to watch Chrissie being punished. I would see her bottom.

The prospect confused me. I was very fond of her but our relationship was primarily based on professional respect and mutual understanding. I was interested enough in girls to appreciate her attractions, but I hadn't harboured the slightest desire for anything more intimate than an occasional gossipy drink after work. I did not really want to witness her being embarrassed and hurt, but on the other hand, my newfound curiosity about bottoms made the thought of seeing hers naked rather enticing, and my heart began to pound.

Then Jonquil shattered my hopes. 'Being spanked is essentially a private thing,' she said solemnly, 'so if you would wait outside, Lucy, I'll deal with Chrissie first.'

I was so disappointed that I just stood there for several seconds, my mouth open. 'Can't I stay and watch?' I blurted clumsily, and my heart sank as the words echoed through my head and I closed my eyes in confident anticipation of an angry denial of my wish and confirmation that I had earned myself extra punishment. But to my relief and delight, Jonquil did no such thing.

'Why not?' she said, with some enthusiasm. 'As long as Chrissie doesn't mind.' We both looked at her.

'As long as I can watch her,' she responded.

I smiled, heaved a huge sigh and tried to get into the right frame of mind for yet another new experience.

I watched Chrissie settle down over Jonquil's lap, holding my breath as her skirt inched smoothly upwards, revealing remarkably shapely legs, then her rounded bottom, and her white knickers gleaming under the stretched nylon of her black tights. These were tugged down easily, and I realised that Chrissie had helpfully lifted up her hips and told myself to remember to do the same when it was my turn.

Jonquil paused as soon as the tights were neatly arranged around Chrissie's knees, and we both stared for several minutes at the seat of her panties.

They were rucked up between her buttocks and the chubby little bits at the base were exposed. I saw that she had lovely long folds where cheek and leg joined.

As Jonquil pulled her knickers down with tantalising deliberation, I emptied my straining lungs as more and more of what even I could see was an exceptionally pretty bottom came into view.

43

Again Jonquil paused when Chrissie's last protection was down to her knees, and I couldn't resist leaning forward for a closer view. My first impression was that her bottom was bigger and chubbier than I'd expected. It quivered beautifully as she settled her weight on Jonquil's thighs, and I finally and fully understood why spanking a pretty girl is so exciting.

The combination of round, smooth, white buttocks; the tight division; the folds at the base and, from my vantage point at least, the tendrils of dark curly hair peeping out underneath was all irresistible.

Then Jonquil got the spanking underway and it all made even more sense. The ringing sound of the spanks; the way Chrissie's bottom wobbled, quivered and bounced; the lovely and ever-changing pink; her gasps and, later on, her little cries of pain. Exquisite.

After a while my curiosity got the better of my discretion and I began to move around, keen to see it all from different angles. Standing by her right side, looking down at her bottom, I noticed how the ripples from the spanks travelled up to her hips and were especially noticeable there.

Moving to her head, I could see her sweet face, screwed up as she absorbed the mounting pain. She gave me a rueful smile and then her eyes glazed over as she concentrated on her bottom. So did I and was entranced by the view, with the steep incline of her naked back sweeping up to her buttocks and the top of her cleft. Her cheeks looked very round and the cleft lovely and tight.

It occurred to me that making a film of a spanking

could be both challenging and very exciting and I kept moving, squinting to see it as though through a lens.

Then the sound of flesh on flesh stopped and I came back to earth with a jolt, realising it was my turn next. Jonquil was smiling at me and I felt my face burn.

'Checking camera angles, Lucy?' she asked.

'Are you a mind reader?' I gasped.

'No – an optimist.'

I was too confused even to try and work out what she meant, especially as she immediately helped a red-faced and red-bottomed Chrissie to her feet and patted her lap in unmistakable invitation.

My third spanking seemed less painful than the second, and obviously couldn't end so thrillingly. Knowing that Chrissie was watching helped me to concentrate on presenting my bottom nicely, and also make as little fuss as possible.

And now that I had a far better idea of what it was like from the other point of view, I found the actual spanking more exciting.

Though the caning that followed was just agonisingly painful!

I had forgotten Jonquil's promise to punish us severely, and so when she ordered us both to strip naked and then Chrissie to move into the middle of the room and grip her ankles, I was horrified.

And it got worse. I could hardly watch as my friend obeyed, walking slowly over to the designated spot, her bright pink bottom standing out like a beacon in contrast to the flawlessly white skin of her back and legs. She stood upright for a while, her shoulders rising and sinking as she took long deep breaths, her buttocks trembling.

Then they changed shape dramatically as she bent over, spreading and separating, her tight cleft opening and the folds disappearing. It all seemed to happen in slow motion as I looked on helplessly, half riveted by the scene, half appalled at the thought of dear Chrissie having to suffer.

Six times the wicked, springy, yellow cane rose, hovered, hummed viciously through the air and thwacked loudly into Chrissie's sweet bare bottom.

Six times she cried out and bent her knees inwards, splaying her buttocks even more.

Six times I caught a glimpse of her anus. It was rude. I should've look away, but couldn't.

Six lines appeared like magic, right across her bottom, pale at first then rapidly swelling and darkening to an angry red.

Then it was over and she straightened up painfully, her hands reaching back to soothe her bottom. Jonquil brusquely ordered her to stand straight and put her hands on her head. Then she crouched down behind her, admiring her handiwork. She expressed satisfaction at the result, gave the weeping girl a forgiving cuddle and then beckoned me.

On shaky legs I took Chrissie's place and reached down for my ankles. I felt the cane rest against the centre of my tight bottom and a scream of fear tried to surface. Then I heard the threatening hum, heard the crisp whack as the first stroke landed, felt the ripple spread through my buttocks and then did scream as a line of fiery agony seared me, exactly where she'd rested the cane.

Jonquil waited until I presented my bottom again, by which time the pain had ebbed away a little, leaving a hot throbbing in its wake.

The second one was a bit easier to take, probably because I knew what to expect and was better prepared. I seized upon every possible distraction to help me; clinging to my ankles, hard enough to hurt; holding my breath until the cane struck me, then expelling it in one gust; remembering that I deserved to be punished; telling myself that Chrissie was watching and I wanted to impress her; trying to imagine how different our bottoms looked; reminding myself that I loved Jonquil…

Then it was over and Jonquil was helping me to straighten up. I was amazingly dry-eyed, but couldn't help hopping around while she inspected my bottom, the pain intensifying as she smoothed her fingertips over my striped cheeks.

But then the burning sting was totally irrelevant.

The door opened and Clive marched in!

Chapter Two

I wasn't really in a position to take in much detail. In fact, it was all I could do to prevent myself passing out. I could hardly draw breath, there was a horrid roaring in my ears and I very nearly threw up. It didn't even occur to me to try and cover up the salient features of my naked front. I just stood there, panting and waiting for Clive to explode, vaguely wondering what sort of reference I could possibly expect after this.

When I think back on those few minutes – which, even now, I can't do without a shudder – I realise that my submissiveness really surfaced. It never occurred to me that it would be logical for Clive to turn any anger on his wife rather than on the two suffering and woebegone members of his staff. I automatically assumed that he would put the blame firmly on me. After all, I was naked, it must have been blindingly obvious that I had just been beaten, and had therefore committed a wrongdoing. And in a state of near shock and considerable discomfort I completely overlooked the fact that Chrissie was also starkers and sporting a striped bottom.

Then my senses cleared a little and I noticed that Clive seemed far more embarrassed than angry, that he was staring unashamedly at my breasts and sex and that he wasn't showing any sign of surprise at what must have been the strangest homecoming of his life.

As I finally got round to moving my shaking hands to cover myself a little, he gave me one of his lovely grins. My heartbeat slowed a little and I managed a weak smile in return. Then I found that I didn't even have the strength to keep my hands in place, and my arms lowered to my sides.

The next few minutes passed in a blur. I vaguely heard him apologise for coming back so unexpectedly and explain that the client had been so enthusiastic about our proposals for their new product development campaign that he'd been able to get away early and hadn't had to spend the night away.

The good news was not only welcome as far as the agency was concerned, but also provided my overloaded brain with the perfect excuse to latch on to something which would allow me to forget most recent events. My nakedness seemed irrelevant all of a sudden, and I immediately began to press him for more details, hoping that I would be able to play a bigger role in the campaign.

'Later, Lucy, all will be revealed.' He then looked pointedly at my body again and the graphic reminder sent me moving quickly for my clothes. 'Oh, no you don't,' he said. 'Far too pretty a sight to be covered up – especially after a long hard day. And a successful one, I hasten to add. I feel I've earned a reward and your naked charms will do nicely. Very nicely.'

I felt myself blushing, still embarrassed and confused but marginally less so after his compliment. Then I realised that when I'd turned to fetch my clothes, he would have seen my bottom. I curled up inside again and stood there in the middle of the room, neither knowing nor caring what was going on around me. I was simply too far gone, so when Chrissie was asked to stand beside me so that Clive could inspect his wife's handiwork, I was hardly aware of her presence.

I heard Clive saying something about one of the weals on Chrissie's bottom not being even or straight, and it took several minutes before the full implications of his remarks struck home; Clive was obviously as enthusiastic an administrator of CP as Jonquil.

I couldn't make up my mind whether that was reassuring or not, so slipped it into neutral and let the two of them get on with it.

Over the next half an hour or so I gradually began to come round and, by the time Clive had suggested a celebratory bottle of champagne, I was feeling less resigned, helped no end by the way the pain in my bottom had been replaced by a delicious glow.

At last we were asked if we would like to get dressed and then stay for supper. Part of me wanted to carry on flaunting myself, but commonsense prevailed and, with the occasional wince as I eased knickers and tights over my bottom, I restored myself to something like normality.

Not that the evening could ever be described as normal. In spite of my efforts to get Clive on to the safer ground of work, he insisted on asking us about our punishment, demanding to know how we'd felt before, during and after.

I reminded him rather tartly that, as far as I was concerned, I hadn't been given the chance to experience the after bit, but he grinned at me, filled my glass with the most delicious champagne and pressed me to carry on.

As the evening progressed I began to lose more of my inhibitions. Obviously the champagne helped, and so did the delicious supper Jonquil conjured up; yet another annoying reminder of her many talents. Even more influential was the way that neither of them showed the slightest self-consciousness about their enthusiasm for punishing girls' bottoms, so it was not surprising that my own newfound enthusiasm began to blossom, especially as the afterglow was still thrilling me.

What finally and irrevocably convinced me that there was nothing intrinsically wrong with gaining pleasure from a spanking was a nice little story Clive told. I can still picture the scene; Clive and Jonquil sitting on the sofa, Chrissie and me in separate armchairs, that large room with the stunning view, Tower Bridge lit up, the glistening river with the occasional boat moving steadily along, a glass of vintage brandy in my hand, my bottom throbbing reminiscently, a warm knot of excitement in the pit of my stomach, and Clive's seductive voice as he told his tale.

'Quite a long time ago, before the National Health Service was established, two GP's were having tea in the garden of the senior one. He had been in practice for thirty years or so, and had all the accumulated knowledge and wisdom you would expect.

'The other was newly qualified and was doing a few months to gain experience of general practice. They were discussing the day's cases and the younger one said that he'd been faced with something rather unusual that morning, in that one of their patients, a stolid farmer, had admitted that he got a strong sexual sensation every time he blew his nose.

"'What did you say to him?" the old boy asked.

"'Basically, that although I'd covered psychiatry at medical school I was hardly an expert, but I'd do what I could to help cure him.

"'Ah," said the older doctor, with enough inflexion in his voice to make the younger realise he hadn't necessarily done the right thing.

"'What would you have said, sir?" he asked.

"'Just that some people have all the luck," the old boy replied wistfully.'

I laughed, but didn't get the real point immediately, and Jonquil saw the little frown on my face. 'Look, Lucy,' she said, 'you like kisses and cuddles, right?'

'Yes, of course.'

'Fine. So as well as all the normal things, you also like having your bare bottom smacked, right?'

'Well, yes,' I replied rather hesitantly, still and despite all the evidence, reluctant to face up to the obvious.

'There you are then,' she mused triumphantly. 'You're lucky.'

I took a contemplative sip of cognac and, as it warmed my tummy, felt a surge of excitement. So I was lucky, and the obvious course was to accept it and offer my bottom with a clear conscience.

Jonquil then told Clive about my watching Chrissie's spanking with a film director's eye, he looked at me with both surprise and respect, and the upshot was that they told me they had a number of friends who shared their tastes for bottoms in general and spanking in particular, and one aspect enjoyed by all was watching videos.

Then the penny dropped. 'And you'd like me to think up some ideas,' I said slowly.

Clive nodded.

'And to direct them,' said Jonquil.

'With our help,' they added simultaneously, and from that moment my life took a dramatic change.

I was able to devote a fair amount of time and effort to the new project over the next couple of weeks as Chrissie was on holiday, and therefore most of the work went to the other creative teams. It did not take me long, however, to realise that I didn't know where to start!

I had never seen a spanking film and only had my own very limited experiences to go on. I couldn't even have a quiet word with Chrissie, although strangely enough, I still felt rather awkward about our one shared beating. Even though she was a good friend and colleague and attractive enough to be desirable to most, our relationship was precious as much as anything because it was something of a change from the sexually charged atmosphere at work. Now that I had seen her bare bottom – and what lay between and below those adorable little cheeks – I found it a bit hard to come to terms with the new sense of intimacy.

So, the obvious answer was to go cap in hand to Jonquil, admit that I was groping in the dark, offer to take her out to dinner and pick her brains.

She greeted my proposal with one of her special grins, refused dinner on the grounds that we would both feel inhibited with strangers in earshot, and insisted that I went round to their flat so that she and Clive could brief me more fully.

I left with hundreds of thoughts and ideas buzzing round my brain, took the next day off, a Friday, to give me the whole weekend to make a start, stocked up with wine and frozen meals and got down to it.

The several commercially available videos they'd shown me left me with quite a few ideas, mainly on how to do a great deal better. While I fully understood that most of them were shot with amateur equipment, probably with a very limited budget and in a hurry, my main impression was that few of them showed much in the way either of imagination or attention to detail. For example, in one with a schoolgirl theme, both miscreants were spanked and then stripped to be caned, and after their punishment they scuttled over to where they had left their clothes and got dressed. The camera totally failed to follow them as they went and missed a golden opportunity to focus on their bare bottoms as they bent down to pick up their knickers.

Having said that, I was amazed at the severity of the punishments in a lot of the films. There were some very red cheeks on display and, by the end, I was completely hooked on spanking, to the extent that I went home wishing Jonquil had put me across her knee, even though Clive was there and I still went red at the memory of the last time.

So I let my mind roam free, trying to think of some

exciting plots. The majority of the videos I had seen were set in some form of school, obviously featuring older girls but still in more or less appropriate uniform. There was something quite exciting about the scenario, and it was clearly popular with the enthusiasts. As Clive had given me some fairly strong hints that he and his circle of friends not only produced videos for their own entertainment but also had a profitable sideline in selling them to others, I had to bear in mind a much wider potential market.

I paced up and down thinking furiously, and kept coming back to the school theme. After a while I began to understand the attraction. Even though I had never been even threatened with a spanking at any of the schools I'd been to, the atmosphere of authority and discipline provided a certain logic, especially given the undeniable historical fact that schools must have provided more opportunities for punishment of naked bottoms than almost any other environment.

So I decided to stick to what was creatively safe ground, but it had to be clear that all the girls were over eighteen.

Therefore it had to be a college of some sort – a specialised place to help girls who had already failed their A-levels and whose parents were more than happy with old-fashioned methods. On that basis, the girls would have been over eighteen anyway and it would not take a great deal of complicated dialogue to emphasise the point.

By the end of the weekend I felt I'd managed to produce something worth showing Clive and Jonquil and, first thing on Monday morning, I handed her a carefully sealed envelope with the plot in some detail, an outline script and a storyboard, giving some idea of camera angles. She was impressed with my efficiency and promised that she would come back to me as soon as possible; although she did warn me that Clive was horrendously busy, so it could well take several days to consider my idea properly.

I was quite glad to get back to normal, especially as I'd been asked to work with one of the other teams on one of our biggest clients, so that I had new problems to get my teeth into. Even so, my mind did drift to images of bare-bottomed girls across the headmaster's lap from time to time, and I found it hard not having anyone to discuss my newfound interest with.

Then Jonquil found an excuse to spank me again, and thankfully the studio was free so I didn't have to hang around for too long.

We went in, locked the door, turned on the warning light and stood looking at each other. I suddenly realised that I had seldom been so wound up. With each of the previous punishments I'd felt nervous, ashamed, a bit confused and very conscious of my threatened bottom, but now that I had a far better idea of the full implications, there was the added element of intense sexual excitement. My nipples were so stiff they were almost painful, and I knew my sex was getting moist. And I was not exactly unhappy to see that Jonquil looked just as stimulated. Her eyes glittered, her tongue kept slipping out and licking her lips, I could see her face and neck were getting pink and, as my eyes followed the spreading flush down to the V-shaped opening in her blouse, saw that her nipples were very prominent.

My heart pounded even more violently as she reached out and rested her hands on my hips, drawing me close enough for her to reach the tight seat of my jeans.

'I'm going to give you a really sound spanking, Lucy,' she breathed, and the hoarseness in her voice sent shivers down my spine. 'On your bare bottom.'

'Yes, Jonquil,' I replied, hoping that the hushed tone of my voice would communicate my feelings.

There was a pause and her voice echoed in my mind as she smiled at me, and I just stood there looking into the swimming depths of her eyes. The thrills grew stronger as my bottom tingled under both the threat and the gentle touch of her hands. My lungs felt constricted, my breathing reduced to shallow pants. Her words were still in my head and I realised what a powerful weapon they can be. Those two short sentences painted such a vivid picture; the pain of a spanking, the nakedness, the inherently humiliating position – I could understand her pleasure in saying them.

Then she was sitting down and I was standing by her knees, watching her slim fingers undoing my belt, freeing the top button, easing the zip down. I began to feel a bit dizzy. She guided me round to her right and I floated across her lap, automatically reaching down to the floor with my hands and shuffling forward until my bottom was in the middle.

Her thighs felt so firmly soft under me.

Her hands got busy with my slackened jeans and I lifted my hips to make it easier for her to take them down. They dragged my knickers down with them. Not far, but the pressure of elastic on the upper curves of my cheeks made it clear that the top inch or so of my bottom cleft was uncovered. I lay there and waited breathlessly for Jonquil to complete the process.

But to my surprise, she not only tugged the waist back into place but also fiddled around with the lower bits, covering my quivering cheeks completely. I frowned, wondering why she didn't strip me immediately. Not that my disillusionment lasted long. I soon cottoned on to the fact that, now she knew I was interested in CP, she felt she could indulge at least some of her baser and more exciting little practices, beginning with a lingering exposure and inspection of the part of me which clearly excited her most.

She tucked the left side of my knickers right into my cleft, leaving one cheek bare and the other covered. Her hands roamed freely over both, obviously revelling in the contrast between covered and bare buttock. Then she bared the other side and again had a good feel.

I felt her hands on my waist and lifted up, enjoying the complimentary little pat before she slowly pulled the elastic over the curves of my buttocks, using those elegant fingers to ease the tucked in bits out of the division.

Hardly surprisingly my head was swimming by the time she finished baring me. I was half longing to be spanked and half dying for her to take as long as she wanted, because just lying there, with my naked front pressing into her soft thighs and knowing that her eyes were glued to my bare bottom was a real thrill.

Eventually I was spanked. And pretty hard, although it seemed to hurt less than previously, and I lay there feeling almost drunk from all the preparations, loving the sound and feel of Jonquil's stiff palm hitting me, my mind drifting between fantasy and reality.

One moment I was completely absorbed by the physical aspects of being spanked, and the next I was imagining how I would direct a film of my spanking, trying to think where to aim the camera. On my bottom, of course, but then I thought it would be interesting to focus on Jonquil's face. And on mine. And which would be the best angles? I desperately tried to remember which viewpoints of Chrissie's spanking had appealed most, but I was on such a high that the details were blurred. Then the growing pain in my poor suffering bottom distracted me.

The obvious solution was to go with the flow and accept my punishment. All I could hear was the pounding of my heart and the rhythmic sound of Jonquil's hand on my bare bottom. I was no longer a bright woman with a growing reputation in a competitive and backstabbing business. I was not even a naughty girl undergoing punishment. I was just a feminine, apparently rather pretty and totally bare bottom.

A sore bottom.

It was at that point that I really began to appreciate the pain of a spanking. Up until then it had been something to shrink from, rather like banging one's head against a wall – lovely when it stopped. Each ringing spank made me see stars and the inexorable accumulation made my poor bottom hotter and hotter until it seemed on the verge of meltdown. And yet there were no tears in my eyes. I was grunting, gasping and whimpering, but not crying out and certainly in no mood to beg her to stop. I found a strange triumph in presenting Jonquil with as stable a target as I could, although I knew that my middle was bobbing up and down on her lap, but even in my pain and confusion I was still aware that I was instinctively moving in perfect tune with the rhythm of her hand. As it landed the impact was enough to press me against her lap, but I immediately lifted my bottom again, openly inviting the next.

I concentrated hard on both the pain and the rhythm, sensing that there was a strange harmony between us. My thoughts suddenly seemed amazingly clear and focused. I revelled in the subtle communication between us. The fact that she obviously adored my bottom no longer disturbed me in the least, and her domination of me suddenly changed from bizarre to utterly natural.

Then and remarkably suddenly, the pain overwhelmed and I burst into a flood of tears as I reached the limit of my endurance. Jonquil immediately stopped spanking me and began to soothe my burning cheeks, whispering something about me having taken my punishment bravely, but to be honest I was far too wrapped up in myself to take a great deal of notice.

I did feel her kiss my buttocks some time later, and the cool softness of her lips left an imprint that lingered even after my flesh had recovered.

The following day I asked her if I could have my proposals back, as I'd come to the conclusion that I'd not come up with anything really original and needed to try to incorporate some of my emotions during the previous day's spanking.

I refined the original plot, gave more thought to the basic direction, asked Jonquil if I could go round to their flat again so she could give me another caning, as the first had been pure punishment and I wanted to see if I would react differently now that I'd made the connection between pain and pleasure.

And I certainly did! Clive's presence made me feel a bit awkward at first, but his tremendous charm, combined with a third of a bottle of champagne, soon had me relaxed. The two of them made it a memorable experience and I emerged with six beautiful red weals decorating my bottom, and much more capable of rising to the challenge of pretty severe pain.

I was soon ready to start shooting the video, and was relieved when Clive volunteered Jonquil's services as producer, as I would have struggled with things like casting and location, but she came up trumps as usual.

The basic plot was as I had originally planned; set in a sort of sixth form college, and with the headmistress having to deal with two erring girls. The first refinement I had come with was to have one girl black and the other white. The second was for one to be very much into CP and the other a complete novice. The third – well, that provided something of a surprise finale to the film, and I'll come to that later.

I had also given quite a bit of thought to how best to capture as many of the exciting elements to witnessing a spanking as possible, and had come up with the obvious conclusion of using two cameras, with Greg operating one and me the other.

I checked the location and made a few changes to allow for easier movement of the cameras, and very nervously one quiet Sunday, we got to work.

Jonquil had selected the three actresses carefully and well. Jenny, the white girl, was very pretty indeed; tall, brunette, with expressive eyes and a smiling mouth and already into the spanking scene, so she could play the part of the experienced girl with ease.

Sarah was equally suitable. She was a rich brown, and her dazzling smile was contagious, so that whenever we were taking five we all did our best to make her laugh. Her bottom was stunning, curving firmly from the small of her back, with a lovely tight cleft and neat little folds at the base of each cheek. It quivered excitingly when it was smacked, and her complexion was light enough to show a change of colour during her spanking, and the cane weals stood out as raised dark lines across her full cheeks.

Jenny's was a little smaller, lovely and white it wobbled rather than quivered, and reddened dramatically.

Susan, who played the headmistress, was undoubtedly the star. In her mid-thirties, she was too plump to interest the fashion industry but had a sexual aura that had my hormones on full alert from the beginning. She also had a lovely face, a fantastic complexion, rich blonde hair, a warm voice and an infectious laugh.

The action started with the two girls walking down a corridor, dressed in short dark blue skirts and white blouses, suggesting school uniforms but no more, with the camera zooming in on a close-up of both skirts, giving a pleasant hint of mobile bottoms underneath. Then they were waiting nervously outside the head's study, with Jenny trying to persuade her friend that they will probably be offered the option of a beating rather than expulsion, and that she would be well advised to take it. 'I'm sure she'll like your bottom,' she added enigmatically, just as the headmistress appeared and ushered them into the study.

She sat at her desk, announced that as they had been caught red-handed smoking pot, there was no point in trying to excuse themselves and so the only item on the agenda was the punishment. As predicted, she offered a beating as an alternative to being expelled, and the white girl agreed with only a slight show of reluctance. The black girl, Sarah, was far less amenable, but gave way in the end.

The headmistress then offered to warm up their bottoms with a moderate spanking, with Jenny going first and Sarah told to watch carefully.

Although these opening minutes were simply to set the scene, I thought hard about building up a sense of anticipation in the audience. First by the close-ups of the girls' skirts, then by showing their reactions as the headmistress sentenced them, with Jenny pouting rather unconvincingly and Sarah looking genuinely frightened, emphasised by a close-up of her nervously twisting fingers.

In complete silence, the camera followed the head's hands as she entered the gory details in the punishment book, cutting briefly to Sarah's eyes widening in genuine horror as she peered over her superior's shoulder and saw the words *twelve strokes* in the penultimate column, and *bare bottom* in the last one.

One camera followed the headmistress purposefully moving her chair from behind the desk to the front, sitting down, smoothing her skirt over her thighs and then pointing to her lap, while the other focused on the girls' faces, with Jenny looking quite composed and Sarah anything but.

When Jenny moved the few paces forward to the waiting lap, I again had one camera focused on the seat of her skirt, the gentle rolling of her hips just discernible and, I hoped, building up a sense of anticipation in the viewer.

As she was used to being spanked, Jenny instinctively bent over Susan's knee with an easy grace, and needed no prompting to get into the right position. As soon as she had settled, Greg and I worked well together to capture what I felt was the first key moment – having her bottom bared. One thing about the commercial videos that had puzzled me was that more often than not, the girls' knickers weren't pulled down until some time after the spanking had started. I eventually worked out that the probable reason was to delay the excitement in seeing their bottoms bare, but I found it unconvincing and rather frustrating. Admittedly, I had very limited experience at that stage, but knowing I was to get it on my bare bottom was a vital element of the build up to the punishment. Even after several spankings, the feeling of my knickers sliding down over my rounded cheeks had always made me curl up inside.

I also felt that if the denuding was done after the spanking had started, most girls would be too wrapped up in their sore bottoms to feel the same way about it.

So, I had written the script accordingly and made quite sure that we made it as dramatic and exciting as possible, again gaining full benefit from the two cameras to capture the expressions on both faces and the actual action as Jenny's smooth bottom came into view. I was certainly pleased with the result.

We got Jenny's flushed face with a view over her right shoulder of her raised middle, so that her bottom was visible as her knickers were eased down to her thighs, then Susan's face shot from slightly below, with Jenny's right buttock in the foreground, and finally a close-up of the exposure, taken from behind and above, catching every little quiver as the knickers slid smoothly down.

Susan helped herself to a good feel of Jenny's rump before she started spanking her. Her expression was subtly eloquent as she looked down on her roving hand, assessing the skin and flesh and discreetly enjoying herself immensely. Then Greg slowly panned in until the screen was completely filled with Jenny's pretty bottom, with Susan's elegant and beautifully manicured hand stroking, squeezing and patting.

Still in close-up, Susan's hand patted the roundest part of Jenny's left cheek, and then disappeared. The mike in my camera picked up Jenny's intake of breath as she realised her spanking was about to begin, and we saw her buttocks twitch anxiously.

Cut to Jenny's face, eyes screwed tight as she bit her lip.

Cut to Susan, her right arm raised, hand stiff, eyes gleaming and a little smile on her face. Then her arm swept down.

Jump cut to the close-up of Jenny's bottom as the hand flashed into view, sank into the soft flesh with a satisfying *crack*, her bottom wobbled beautifully, the hand fell away, leaving a fleeting impression of a white mark on the skin, as Jenny briefly clenched her cheeks in reaction to the sting. We lingered for a second or two, watching the pink mark develop and then cut to my camera to show Jenny's face, her eyes widening as the spank landed and her dry lips parted in a silent 'ow'.

When I edited the film, I decided to use slow motion repeats every so often, unashamedly inspired by Greg's tape of Sharon's walking bottom, and chose the above sequence as an ideal way of introducing the film. The same spank was shown twice more, first at half speed and then cranked right down, with amazing results considering it hadn't been that hard. The way Jenny's buttock was so dramatically distorted by Susan's hand was amazing, and I finished off by freezing the best frame, showing her tight little cleft being forced open and her anus in full view.

As far as the gimmicks went, that was it for the rest of her spanking. Greg shifted his position from time to time, moving from a nice viewpoint at Jenny's feet, to another looking down more or less over Susan's shoulder, and the different perspectives of the suffering bottom were splendidly portrayed, while I tended to concentrate on a side view, most of the time standing well back, taking in both participants and keeping well out of Greg's way. I remember thinking at the time that this was an excellent angle, as it showed so many of the different elements of a spanking, from the submissive curve of Jenny's body lying gracefully across Susan's lap, to the facial expressions of both. It was also a pleasing view of her bottom, as I was high enough to show the cleft as well as the rather sexy ripples up to her hipbone.

When her bottom was a lovely bright pink, Jenny was told to get up.

'It's time to warm you up, Sarah,' Susan announced, beckoning the cringing girl with an imperious forefinger.

Greg zoomed in to Jenny's bottom as she clambered to her feet and rubbed it with exaggerated fervour, making it wobble beautifully, then to a nice freeze-frame with her clutching both cheeks, fingers sinking into the soft flesh, indenting it under them and causing it to bulge between them.

Then we concentrated on Sarah's preparations, with her far more clumsy approach to and over Susan's knee making her lack of experience and willingness very clear.

She played her part nicely, whimpering when her knickers were pulled down and tightening her buttocks all through the preliminary exploration. The first spank was repeated at the various speeds, with the tension in Sarah's muscles very evident by the much less vivid reaction.

I enjoyed the sight of a white hand on a black bottom so much that, when I edited it, I put fewer of my side and head shots into the final sequence, although there was enough of her face to show that she reacted for more to the pain than Jenny had.

When Sarah had been warmed up the headmistress couldn't resist a lingering look at her handiwork, and so had the two miscreants standing side by side, skirts up and knickers down, and crouched behind them, inspecting closely. The final shot of the sequence was of just the two contrasting bottoms and Susan's face.

To add some variety to the caning action, Susan suggested dividing it into three parts, making the girls adopt different positions for each. For the first four strokes, they bent over the top of her desk with their legs together and straight. For the second, they were made to move their feet apart and bend their knees in, so that their cheeks were rounder, their clefts more open and their fannies showing. The final four were given with them bending right over and clutching their parted ankles, again with knees bent. This not only revealed even more, but as Susan as the headmistress explained, 'will make it harder for you to sway forward.'

She then announced the procedure to the girls, with one camera following the action from the side so that all three faces were in frame, while the other focussed on the pair of pink bottoms, catching each nervous twitch as Susan went into detail. Jenny moved to the desk and bent over with practiced ease, and the cameras captured her first four strokes from several positions, from straight behind, from near Susan's side, and from the other side to bring the girl's face into shot.

The four strokes landed with sizzling accuracy on the upper slopes of her bottom, and she took them bravely.

Then she stood up, grimacing with pain and rubbing her bottom. She stepped back and a wide-eyed Sarah took her place. We filmed her bending over from two angles, one directly behind and the other in front, so that the eventual audience could enjoy both the nervous look on her face and the way her lovely bottom changed shape. Susan had to guide and cajole her before her position was right, and the first stroke had her standing up, wailing in pain and clutching her bottom. But she got better and braver with experience.

Then we saw both bottoms in close-up from a few feet before following Jenny's back to the desk. The main shot of her bending over was taken from behind and fairly low down, so we saw the way her bottom curved dramatically as it swelled out from her thighs, and got a lovely view of her neat and almost hairless sex when she tucked her knees under the desk. The next four strokes landed across the middle of her bottom.

It was Sarah's turn for stage two, and the loom of her bottom when seen from below was stunning. She took her four with more noise than Jenny, but well enough to earn a complimentary remark from the headmistress.

Change places again and it was bent right over. Jenny's little bottom-hole was clearly visible when the camera was right behind her, and we shifted the angle a bit to keep it more modestly hidden.

Sarah took her last four as well as Jenny did. The one slightly disappointing element to her performance was that when the last stroke landed she sprang upright and capered about, wailing and clutching her wealed bottom, to the extent that we failed to capture her movements properly and the impact of the scene was lessened.

Both wriggling girls were made to stand with their faces to the wall for a few minutes, 'to think about the wages of sin', before being told to pull up their knickers and go.

Then we cut to a typical teenage bedroom, with posters on the walls, clothes scattered liberally among textbooks, tapes, CD covers and varied sporting accessories. Both bottoms were carefully bared and cold cream applied liberally.

Fade to the head's study again, clearly after dark with the curtains drawn and lights on, and with the good lady working at her desk.

We cut again, this time to Jenny's rear view as she walked sinuously down the corridor, and with a zoom into the tight seat of her pyjamas as she went straight into the study without knocking, up to the desk, and the two participants smiled at each other.

The ensuing dialogue made it clear that poor Sarah had been set up. Jenny and the headmistress had an arrangement that if the girl could con one of her colleagues into accepting a thrashing, she could do the same to Susan.

So Jenny sat down, took Susan across her lap, pulled her nightie up to her waist, enjoyed a lingering feel of her lush bare bottom and then spanked it soundly. Then the headmistress was made to strip naked, take Jenny's pyjamas off and submit to a three part caning.

We faded out on a recovering headmistress kissing her pupil, while both pairs of hands kneaded two pairs of naked, striped buttocks.

I was able to take my time over the editing, and so it wasn't until about three weeks after shooting that all Clive and Jonquil's likeminded friends gathered in their flat for the premiere. Not surprisingly, I was a bundle of nerves. I usually was when presenting a film I'd been involved with, especially the first showing to the relevant people at the agency, who tended to be even more critical than the client.

That evening was considerably worse, probably because I carried sole responsibility and didn't even have the usual escape clause of a muddled brief from the client, but the reception that greeted the video first and me afterwards will stay in my memory for the rest of my life.

Even I had to admit the film was good. Greg had been a brilliant leader of the actual shooting, and the use of the best and most sophisticated equipment we could get helped a lot.

The lighting was excellent, which was not that easy as we had to set it up for several camera positions and angles, and yet could hardly interrupt the spanking action to make adjustments.

The actresses were amazingly good, bearing in mind that none of them were professional. Admittedly, I had taken this into account and kept the script to a minimum, and discouraged them from extemporising, clearly remembering that Jonquil had always concentrated on spanking me and I had concentrated on being spanked. Once I was bared and bent, there had been little need for conversation.

The scene that probably worked best of all was the

build up to the headmistress submitting to Jenny. The girl looked sweet and sexy in her pyjamas. Susan took off her dressing gown as soon as she had locked the door and revealed herself in the sexiest nightie I had ever seen, in sheer black nylon, her pale body contrasting deliciously.

When the large screen went blank I looked round anxiously, and the approving looks on all the faces came as a huge relief. I had been too involved with looking for the bits which hadn't worked as well as planned to take much notice of the audience's reaction, but when they called for an immediate repeat I was able to sit back and watch my work in a much more relaxed frame of mind, and found I was quite turned on, especially by Susan, and resolved to get in touch with her soon. I really wanted to get to know her in general, and her gorgeous bottom in particular.

After the second showing, Clive and Jonquil opened several bottles of champagne, pointed out the array of delicious food in the kitchen and, as we all ate and drank, I found myself happily basking in unaccustomed attention, leavened by a few constructively critical comments.

I soon felt very much at home. All the guests were intelligent, sensitive and with an un-British openness about their sexual preferences. Several asked me about my own CP experiences, and I found myself describing them uninhibitedly, although with a little embarrassment when I realised that I was still very much a novice by their standards.

So when Jonquil suggested that it would round the

evening off perfectly if I took a good spanking in front of everybody, I agreed.

First of all I had to stand in the middle of the room with my skirt up, panties around my knees, and allow them all to inspect my bottom closely. That was fine for the first couple, but then Greg came up and, after fondling my cheeks in the same way that his predecessors had done, asked me to touch my toes. It didn't occur to me that he wanted to re-examine his original playground until I felt his thumbs dig into my buttocks and pull them apart, by which time it was too late to protest, and with my face burning I let him get on with it, comforting myself with the thought that his head would probably be masking the more intimate details from the others.

Then I began to find it all very exciting. I should have felt embarrassed, humiliated and degraded at being treated like an animal at a market, standing meekly while a group of relative strangers helped themselves to as many gropes of my bottom that they wanted, but I didn't – I revelled in it.

Then Jonquil found a suitable chair, sat down, put me across her knee, told everyone to take up a good vantage point as quickly as they could, then gave me a prolonged spanking. I immediately noticed that she was setting about me in a very different way; she was spanking me quite a bit faster and much less crisply than when she had been punishing me, and I soon appreciated both the difference and the results, in that although I could feel my buttocks steadily getting warm, the sting was only just enough to make things interesting, without causing me the slightest distress. At the same time she was

73

hitting me hard enough to make my bottom wobble nicely, and with my newfound experience as an observer, I could easily see that we were providing her friends with a pretty sensual spectacle. It did not escape my notice that when she swept her hand upwards, skimming it over the cheeks rather than driving her palm stingingly into the flesh, the effect on my most sensitive parts was marked.

Even so, I was eventually quite sore, extremely turned on and, according to one and all, the proud possessor of a lovely red bottom.

After a brisk rub and close inspections by all interested parties, I had cooled down enough to want more. When I looked back on it all later, I was amazed how far I had advanced in a relatively short time, although I had to admit to myself that the heady atmosphere, coupled with a fair amount to drink, had made my normal inhibitions faintly ridiculous and the warm glow in my bottom was definitely turning me on. There was a nice big footstool by one of the sofas and I stripped naked, moved it into the middle of the room and knelt up on hands and knees, sticking my bottom out invitingly.

'Six from each of you, please,' I said boldly, looking back over my shoulder and smiling at the sight of all those eyes staring at me with avid approval.

I shudder to think how I would have felt if nobody had showed the slightest inclination to spank me. I would have died, but as it was they sorted themselves out, typically ladies first and hosts last, then the first approached, her eyes sparkling and a broad smile on her face. I watched her bending over my raised bottom until the crick in my neck forced me to face my front, but I remembered her name was either Jane or Anne, and that she was a doctor.

After all present had given me the requested six I tottered to my feet, puffing and blowing and ruefully rubbing a pretty sore bottom before finding my clothes and getting dressed. My glass was refilled and the next hour passed quickly. I felt great. Everyone was as complimentary about my bottom as they had been about the film, and I was again struck by everyone's open enthusiasm for spanking and bottoms and their total lack of any guilt.

Three of the guests made a particularly strong impression. First there was the doctor – it was Jane. She had the most gorgeous blue eyes, honey-blonde hair and an infectious laugh. She also said some rather nice things about my bottom, which I did find a little embarrassing but didn't feel that I knew her anything like well enough to ask what was so fascinating about it.

Another guest who made a more vivid impression was Morganna. To be honest, she frightened the life out of me and I was glad I wasn't alone with her. She was over six feet tall, with long, very black hair. Her skin was startlingly white, with bright red lipstick adding dramatic emphasis. She moved with deliberate grace and there was something about her that reminded me of a deadly snake. Not that she said or did anything to threaten me during the evening; she hadn't even smacked my bottom especially hard, but I kept catching her scrutinising eye and her enigmatic smile whenever our glances crossed, which sent a shiver down my spine.

One of the men present was much more reassuring. His name was Roger, he was in his forties, darkly handsome, and he shared Clive's air of calm authority. His smile was full of warmth and his comments on my video were thoughtful and constructive. We had several little chats, and when he caught my eye my tummy tingled with excitement.

All too soon it was late, so I got a taxi back to my flat, rubbed cream into my beaten bottom, and slept like a log.

Rather disturbingly, it took me several days to get over the reaction to what had been a pretty earthshattering evening. I suppose that was understandable, really; there I was, with a fairly conventional background and with enough Irish ancestry to provide an innate sense of guilt to go with my red hair and unpredictable temper, suddenly with a reputation for producing the sort of videos those ancestors would have roundly condemned – in public, anyway.

For the few days following the 'premiere', I was very jumpy, as though expecting any one of my colleagues to leer knowingly at me over the photocopier, and every unexpected knock on the front door at home made me jump. I even had dreams of visits from an obscene publications squad, one of which ended with me being bent over for a sound thrashing on my bare bottom.

But nothing unpleasant did happened.

I really missed Chrissie, sensing she was the only person I could properly confide in, but when she eventually got back the two of us were thrown together in a frantic pitch for a new client, so I was far too busy for any more silly worries, and for a few days at least sex, spanking and videos were put right to the back of my mind.

The pitch proved to be both challenging and absorbing, and not for the first time I thanked my lucky stars that I'd been teamed up with Chrissie. Her calm intelligence was a perfect foil for my often wayward flights of fancy, and between us we eventually came up with a campaign concept the client liked, to the extent that we won the account, which was big enough to make a significant difference to the agency's fortunes.

The client was a car manufacturer, Japanese but with an assembly plant in England, and the actual product was a new super-mini that, according to their marketing team, was significantly ahead of the opposition in terms of performance, practicality, reliability and economy. They also admitted quite openly that it looked a bit like a dog's breakfast and therefore lacked showroom appeal, which didn't exactly make it easy to make a good initial visual impact in the advertising.

Chrissie and I flicked through our own marketing department's mass of statistics on perceived consumer characteristics, demographic profiles, decision criteria etc. and then decided to go our own way. The clients were happy to lay on a demonstration of the car at a remote airfield, and after a detailed look round the car's interior, we took it in turns to blast it up and down the runway and through a variety of curves to test the handling. We also did our reputation no harm at all by having had the forethought to bring a whole lot of bits with us, from several shopping bags to a child's pushchair, so we could put the practical aspects to a proper test.

In the end we were both very impressed, and we set off for home in thoughtful mood, knowing it would be difficult to get the car's many strong points across when we knew that nobody was going to buy it for its looks.

In the end we went for subtlety rather than high production values. We used a garage for the location, and scripted what was basically a talking heads commercial with just a low-key salesman and a typical nineties busy mother, with no time for anything other than a straightforward and patently honest sales pitch.

Clive agreed to spend some money on a video to get our ideas across, Greg and I shot it in a couple of days, and we went in to the presentation in our usual state of nervous excitement.

We came out two hours later with mixed feelings – as usual. The problem is basically that there is nearly always dissension in the client's ranks. More often than not some want something that will win prizes for creativity, whereas the more sober want commercials that simply hammer home the sales message.

In that particular campaign Chrissie and I felt we'd come pretty close to pleasing both elements. While the dialogue was relatively hard-hitting and concentrated on the practical qualities, we put in one or two jump cuts of the car being thrown around a circuit, sliding round the corners and being extremely noisy and dramatic. Anyway, we got the impression that our pitch had been different to the others they'd seen, and Clive was quietly confident.

While we were waiting, Chrissie and I worked on different accounts and I didn't see nearly enough of her. We managed to meet up for after work drinks a couple of times, but never on our own, so I was unable to tell her about the video and my strange behaviour at the first showing.

What with my increasing frustration over my inability to take my relationship with Chrissie further into the realms of intimacy, the agonising wait to see of our pitch had been successful and my unease over my interest in spanking, it's hardly surprising that Jonquil found a good excuse to spank me again; for being unnecessarily blunt with a client. She agreed he was a pain in the arse, but it was our job to tolerate such clients.

So, into the studio we went after yet another agonising wait until it was free, and by the time I went across her knee I had come to the slightly bitter conclusion that I could no longer deny my need to be punished properly from time to time. As she tugged my jeans and knickers down, the feeling of cool air on the naked skin of my trembling bottom took my breath away, and the sound and sharp sting of the first few spanks cleared my mind of all doubts and uncertainties.

It hurt, and I felt acutely aware of my bare bottom and of her beautiful eyes upon it. Her thighs felt lovely underneath me and knowing that my naked sex was only inches away from hers added a wicked little tingle to the pain spreading through my buttocks.

I also knew that I deserved to be punished and that having my bare bottom soundly spanked was easily the best way of correcting me. Afterwards I would feel not only cleansed mentally but would be glowing physically for some time, and would feel much more at ease with myself.

As I lay across her lap, gasping and panting, my bottom quivering, I knew I was going to produce more spanking videos, and the thought of producing the car commercial didn't excite me nearly as much.

When Jonquil finally finished I burst into tears, which worried her a little until I was able to confess that it wasn't because she'd been too severe, which she understood completely, and I set off home in a very different mood.

As I said, we won the account, and the celebrations were memorable to say the least.

And then, unbelievably, my lottery numbers came up, and I'd won a million quid, give or take the odd few thousand.

Yours truly was rich!

Chapter Three

With a large glass of white wine in my hand, I walked out onto the patio, sank down on the bench just outside the sitting room, took a restorative mouthful, closed my eyes, listened happily to the silence, and took stock.

I was shattered. The past three months had been hectic to say the least, and the thought of a break from it all was sheer bliss.

It had all started when I broke the news of my big win to Clive and Jonquil, feeling that they were the only people wealthy enough to give me practical advice, and it proved to be one of my better decisions.

Their sympathetic probing soon brought out what I really wanted for my immediate future, bearing in mind that although a million quid seemed at first an absolute fortune, if I'd gone ahead with my initial plans to buy a decent flat in one of the better parts of London, I would have had damn all left over. Therefore a manageable cottage in the country would be a far better bet.

'But what about commuting to work?' I protested, remembering those horror stories about trains delayed because of unsuitable leaves on the line and that sort of twaddle.

At that point Clive came up with his bombshell. Apparently he and some of the group of friends I'd met at the screening of my video owned a company that distributed specialised sex videos, and my first effort was doing very well. At the same time, the agency would hate to lose my services. Therefore, why didn't I work for them on a freelance basis, concentrating mainly on new business pitches and spend the rest of my working time and efforts on the videos? In which case I could keep in touch with the agency via e-mail, phone and fax, commute only when strictly necessary, and enjoy the peace and quiet of the country.

My income from the agency would stay very much the same on average, I would have the interest from a reasonable amount of invested capital, my expenses would be less, and if my videos were as successful as everyone expected, I would be doing very nicely thank you.

It seemed worth a try, so I agreed. Clive and Jonquil sprang into action, and almost before I could draw breath I was looking over a property in Kent, which a friend of theirs wanted to sell. It had originally been a woodman's cottage and so was very isolated and private, which was such a nice contrast to the hurly-burly of London that I was won over even before we'd looked around. It had been beautifully converted, had six or seven acres of the surrounding woods as part of the deal and, best of all, a restored barn, which not only provided ample garage and storage room, but the roof space had been made into a spacious studio.

My worries that the isolation would make me feel vulnerable were largely answered by the existence of a new wire fence all round the property, and remotely operated steel gates guarding the drive. These had been cleverly placed out of sight of anyone going along the lane and, as the entrance to the drive itself looked like a simple farm track, the chances of any non-locals taking an interest were pretty remote.

Sold to the lady with the red hair.

With no buying chain or mortgage to delay things, aided by Clive's charm and energy, I was the proud owner in two weeks and suddenly faced with the horrendous task of furnishing it. Once again Clive and Jonquil came to the rescue. We did a blitz of all the local second hand furniture shops we could find, and in a remarkably short space of time all the basics were in place, with only curtains to complete the picture.

Apart from saving me a small fortune, the joy of buying everything piecemeal was that the end result looked much more appropriate than if I'd gone to an interior designer and ended up with a beautifully co-ordinated but ultimately rather soulless showpiece. Within a couple of days, I really felt at home.

It was a lovely warm spring evening and I breathed in the sweet air, listened to the sounds of the birds and the gentle rustling of the new leaves on the trees, and felt the tension drain slowly away. I began to contemplate ideas for the second spanking video, but frankly it was too much effort. I preferred to anticipate a visit from Chrissie, who had invited herself for the weekend. In the meantime there were meals to plan, books and pictures to put away and hang up, and a start to be made on my new life.

Chrissie certainly made an impact. I had waiting with growing impatience for Friday to pass, and as she was driving down and so had all the problems of London traffic to cope with, I didn't expect her to arrive until at least eight o'clock. The weather had changed from warm and sunny to overcast and sultry, and when I heard an impatient hooting from the gates soon after six o'clock, I was still in a pair of disreputable shorts, an old T-shirt, and hadn't even had a shower. Cursing her for taking me by surprise I opened the gates, heard her car approaching the house, pressed the button to shut us off from the outside world, and had just got to the front door when she drew to a halt.

To my huge relief she looked even scruffier than I did. Obviously she'd not had any client meetings, as she was dressed in the standard creative department rig of jeans and T-shirt, and two hours or so of slow moving traffic on a hot afternoon had reduced her to a weary mess.

Not that I minded at all; I was just pleased that she hadn't shown me up. And even that rather unworthy thought only lasted a couple of seconds, as she clambered wearily out of the car, gave me a rueful grin, a lovely warm kiss and then turned slowly round, her mouth slightly open as she took in my new surroundings, while I looked at her, smiling happily and realising that I really had missed her.

'This is just perfect, Lucy,' she breathed.

'I know,' I agreed modestly.

'And can people wander round?'

'Um, no,' I said, puzzled as to what she was getting

at. 'It's all fenced off.'

'Oh *good*,' she enthused with a cheeky little grin, and started taking her clothes off.

For a moment I wasn't sure whether to laugh or stop her, and by the time I worked out that after her journey, the combination of privacy and fresh air made nudity irresistibly tempting, she was tugging her jeans and knickers down. So I stood watching avidly while Chrissie tossed her clothes onto the bonnet of her car and stood side on to me, her arms stretched out to the side, her eyes closed and a dreamy little smile on her face.

And she looked gorgeous. In profile her breasts and bottom really showed well, as did her shapely thighs. Her skin gleamed in the subdued light and I immediately wished I had a camera to capture both the light and the pose and give me a permanent reminder of the moment.

She broke the spell after several minutes by lowering her arms, taking several deep breaths and then turning to me with a broad grin. 'Come on, Lucy, what are you waiting for?'

'Yes, ma'am,' I replied, grinning back and feeling a bit confused but excited as I tore my things off and threw them on top of hers. Looking back, it's not really surprising that I was finding it all a bit strange; if discovering that Chrissie also accepted CP from Jonquil had been reassuring, the fact that I'd enjoyed watching her being spanked had been more than a little disturbing, but also directly led me into directing the video. At that moment, as we surveyed each other's nudity, I began to wonder if my brief flirtations with other members of my own sex had definitely sowed the seeds of real desire and had not been isolated experiments.

Another surprise was the way Chrissie was behaving. Far from being my intelligent but rather modest friend, she was showing clear signs of being a closet slut, which was something of a blow; I had always thought myself quite a good judge of character.

'Very nice,' she said, as she examined my front. I felt my nipples pucker under both her gaze and flattering approval.

'Thank you, ma'am,' I simpered, curtseying.

'My pleasure.' She grinned again and her eyes glinted mischievously. 'Now turn round so I can look at your bum.'

I felt my face burn as I did so, reminded of being put on display at Clive and Jonquil's flat.

Her hand rested lightly on my right buttock and I jumped. Then she began to stroke and squeeze, and it was so nice I began to relax completely. Soon she had me purring and, when she turned me round to face her, I fell into her arms with a little moan of desire. Our lips met and we were kissing with real passion. I really was extremely turned on and my hands began to roam freely, revelling in her soft smooth skin. Her buttocks felt amazingly cool and her tight cleft deliciously warm as I wriggled two fingertips into it.

Then she pushed away and we looked at each other, smiling rather self-consciously. 'Lucy, I really do need a bath or a shower after that horrible journey,' she said.

'Oh, yes, of course,' I blurted, somewhat shocked by the irrational feeling of rejection I experienced.

If Chrissie had already shown she was capable of

behaving immodestly, the shower opened my eyes to more of her hidden capabilities. First of all she soaped me from top to toe, which was very nice indeed. She even made me bend right over so she could attend to my little anus, which was even nicer, although I was still naïve enough to find it a bit embarrassing. Then she made me stand to one side, took the shower head down, fiddled with it and then sprayed the soap off, and when she crouched between my parted legs and directed the water straight up at my sex and the lower parts of my bottom, the amazing tingling surge had me gasping for breath and very nearly coming.

Then she restored the head to its hook and made me do the same to her, which I enjoyed just as much. Even delving between her buttocks and feeling her tight little anus under my fingertips was a delicious thrill.

The first real sign of our compatibility came immediately after we dried each other. I know Chrissie was just as turned on as I was, but we silently agreed that there was no need to rush too far too quickly. We had all the time we wanted.

There was now an evening chill outside, but we both wanted to savour the fresh air, so we threw on T-shirts and nothing else, went downstairs, opened the bottle of champagne I'd bought as a special welcome for her, sat on the cushioned chairs on the patio, and chatted.

I really enjoyed it. She brought me up to date with all the agency and industry gossip, we discussed campaigns past and present, and generally behaved like best friends.

I had a couple of juicy rib-eye steaks marinating in red wine, with a judicious seasoning of herbs and garlic, and when the light began to fade we slipped back inside, and while I looked after the meat Chrissie prepared a salad and opened a bottle of wine from the case Clive had given me as a housewarming present.

With the good food, good wine, soft lights and gentle music, the atmosphere slowly became sexually charged again. While we were washing up Chrissie reached up to put the wineglasses in one of the wall units, and as she stretched her T-shirt rose enough to uncover the lower part of her bottom, and I just happened to be looking in her direction to make sure she had the right shelf. The sight of her rounded cheeks peeking saucily out from under the hem made me catch my breath, but I carried on at the sink, feeling a little dizzy and determined to take charge of events, in the very near future at least.

Then she had to bend down to put the saucepans on the bottom shelf of one of the floor units, so I stooped quickly and got an enticing view of her sparsely furred quim.

Unable to resist any longer, as soon as we'd finished I pulled her close, kissed her and then put my hands on her bare buttocks, under her shirt. They felt lovely – warm, satiny, soft and yielding but firm at the same time. Chrissie just stood there while I indulged myself, a contented little smile on her face, and then she must have realised that I wasn't sure what to do next, because she began to take charge. Not in a dominating way, but gently leading me towards an appreciation of the real joys of making love with another girl. My previous experiences had really been little more than experimental fumbles, and we started off on much the same basis, going into the sitting room, tossing a couple of cushions onto the floor, stripping off our T-shirts, lying down on our sides, facing each other, and then kissing and stroking until we were incredibly turned on.

Chrissie moved me onto my back, knees up and parted, waiting with bated breath for her to continue – and I wasn't disappointed. She slowly built me up towards the most amazing climax I'd ever had, while I just lay there, eyes closed, hands over my face, breathing disjointedly in absolute bliss.

She started by simply letting her hands roam freely about me, sometimes close together and at others wide apart, so that one minute both my breasts were being stroked and kneaded, and the next she was running the ball of a thumb over my mouth and using her other hand to tickle the insides of my thighs.

I just lay back and wallowed in the attention.

'Christ, you're juicy,' she cooed, and then sensually sucked her finger, which I found incredibly sexy as I looked up at the dreamy expression on her face. 'Juicy Lucy,' she giggled, and then before I could even begin to tick her off for being cheeky, she wriggled round a bit, lowered her head and began to taste between my thighs.

I'm a bit ashamed to confess, but that was the first time I'd ever had my sex properly licked. One of my boyfriends quite enjoyed kissing me down there, but he'd never gone about it properly, and so Chrissie's attentions came as a joyous revelation. I had already suspected that she was more experienced than me, and so I wasn't exactly surprised that she was teaching me so many new things, but the sheer physical thrill of it had me tossing my head from side to side.

Then, just as I was on the verge of coming, she stopped and slithered between my quivering thighs until she was lying on top of me, and I gazed up at her lovely face and whimpered something about her being a cruel and heartless bitch.

Her eyes widened. 'That's not at all nice, Juicy,' she teased. 'I might have to spank you for that.'

'Oh no, please don't,' I whispered. The last thing I wanted at that moment was a spanking, but then she forced a hand underneath me and began to squeeze my bottom rhythmically, and the thought of a relatively mild spanking began to appeal. The little minx must have seen a softening in my expression, as she grinned down at me.

'On second thoughts, I'll save your bottom till later,' she said, and I felt both relief and a tinge of disappointment.

Then she kissed me passionately. My nostrils flared at the taste and smell of my own juices on her lips and tongue, and the waves began pound through my body again until I was once more on the verge, when she disengaged, flipped me over and began to nibble the cheeks of my bottom, stroking my back and legs at the same time.

I was putty in her expert hands and so turned on that I was totally incapable of rational thought. I just felt this amazingly strong sense that I had probably found what I'd subconsciously been looking for. And when she eventually took me over the brink and as, sometime afterwards, I was lying sprawled and limp, I knew that whatever else happened to me, I would always want Chrissie close to hand.

I made a move towards her gorgeous breasts, but she stopped me, said that she was quite happy to wait, held me close and, while I revelled in her smooth nakedness, told me how beautiful I was. Needless to say, I glowed at her praise, relaxed in her arms and really began to unwind. Then we drifted upstairs, and the fact that I'd made up the bed in the spare room was completely irrelevant. We were going to share mine and I crashed out in her arms, utterly content and fulfilled.

We woke up together in the morning, nice and early and with the comforting thought that we had both Saturday and Sunday to cement our burgeoning relationship. I told her I'd bought a guidebook for the local area, and that there were quite a few places well worth a visit, with Bodiam Castle highly recommended by the nice lady in the local shop. Then we realised it was pouring with rain, and decided we'd be better off staying indoors. Of course, neither of us minded one little bit, especially as the cottage had very effective central heating so that we didn't have to wear an awful lot to combat the chill. In fact, after we'd had another deliciously intimate shower, we agreed that nothing at all was best.

As we wandered about, preparing and then clearing away breakfast, I found I couldn't keep my eyes off Chrissie's naked charms.

I had wanted to find out more about her experiences,

both at Jonquil's hands and elsewhere. Before she came I'd been determined to tell her all about the video and show it to her. I wanted her opinion, not just as a friend with what I hoped were similar tastes, but also as an experienced judge of film as a communication medium. Had I managed to get across the excitement of CP? Clive and Jonquil's friends had been complimentary, but I didn't know them well enough to gauge their honesty and suspected that their obvious good manners stopped them being too critical.

But by lunchtime it looked bright enough to go out, and both of us were keen to explore my new surroundings. Flinging on the habitual jeans and jumpers, we jumped into my other major acquisition – a lovely little sports car – and found our way to Bodiam, which proved to be quite a find. The basic structure of the original castle was intact, and enough of the interior walls were still more or less standing to give some idea of the original layout.

And best of all, we could climb to the top of a couple of the towers in the four corners and get a good view of the river. To get up there required an awkward climb up a horribly narrow spiral staircase, with the stone steps worn by the passage of countless feet over the years, and the narrowness making passing people coming down extremely difficult. I made the mistake of going first, Chrissie failed to resist the temptation to tweak my bottom and my anguished squeaks echoed alarmingly. Still, the view was worth it, and except for one rather nerve-wracking place where there was only a rather rusty grill between us and the moat a long way below, it was great.

A little after we were standing in the courtyard, trying to work out the original layout, when Chrissie suddenly took over my role as the romantic fantasist and began to describe an imaginary public whipping of some poor erring servant.

'They would probably do it over there,' she surmised with grisly relish. 'Tie her over a barrel or to a ladder, lash her bare bottom with a heavy strap, with everybody summoned to watch.'

We stood there thoughtfully for several minutes, with me shuddering at the thought of the whole community being made to watch my bottom being bared, bent and beaten for some minor crime. Chrissie was just starting to describe the serving wench so vivid in her mind's eye when a group of kids appeared noisily on the scene, and grinning conspiratorially at each other, we set off to look for a decent pub for lunch.

I had absolutely no sense of doubt as we travelled home, chatting animatedly about nothing in particular. Far from it – I was more content than I could remember having been in the whole of my life. From friend and respected colleague, Chrissie had become far and away the best lover I had ever known, and my thoughts were dwelling on having her naked body under my control, trying to recall exactly how she'd thrilled me so much, in the reasonable hope that I could do something similar to her.

We got home just as there was an ominous roll of thunder, and we only just made it through the front door before the heavens opened. I made us a pot of tea, put some biscuits on a plate, and we carried on talking. Then she took the wind clean out of my sails.

'I'm going to give you a really hard spanking, Juicy,' she announced, as calmly as if she was telling me she was going to pour another cup of tea.

I gaped at her, swallowed convulsively and eventually managed to ask her why.

'For not telling me about the video,' she said, and I noticed there was real anger in her eyes. I fidgeted like a child as I desperately tried to collect my wits. Basically, I didn't want to be spanked by Chrissie. Jonquil had been different, and as the fear and the pain of her punishments had faded from my memory, I'd reckoned that as I was no longer a full-time member of the staff, I would be spared any more serious sessions across her knee. I had perhaps dreamt of the occasional light-hearted smacking, but no more than that. But Chrissie was deadly earnest, and my initial feelings were that I resented the suggestion that I would quietly submit to her. She was my equal, not my superior.

On the other hand, my innate sense of guilt and a childhood being taught that sins must be confessed and atoned for had left a deep and lasting impression. My only real defence was that I hadn't been sure whether our joint punishment had been a one off, or something similar to my routine with the awesome Jonquil, and so I was inherently worried that my active interest in CP would have put her off me for good.

I explained in halting sentences, and when I finished she nodded gravely.

'That's fair enough,' she said thoughtfully, and I

breathed a sigh of heartfelt relief. 'But, you know me well enough to have sounded me out. Apart from feeling betrayed, I would love to have been involved in the film.'

'I really am sorry, Chrissie,' I apologised sincerely. 'I did want to, and if you hadn't been away so much during that time I know I would have confided in you. I Promise. And we can work together on the next one. In fact, I really could do with some help. I can't think of a really exciting plot and would love to have you as a sounding board.'

She thought for a while, the tension building. 'Okay, it's a deal,' she said with an encouraging smile, and I began to relax.

'So you're not going to spank me?' I asked, with as much confidence as I could muster.

'Oh, yes I am,' she replied firmly.

'But I've said I'm sorry,' I wailed. 'And tried to explain. Why do you still have to smack me?'

She reached out, took a firm grip of my chin, turned my head so I was looking straight into her eyes and couldn't fail to see her grim determination.

'For several reasons,' she told me. 'One, you deserve it; we had all last night and today for you to say something. Two, you're the sort of girl who needs to be spanked regularly to keep you in order. And last but by no means least, I've been longing to feel my hand striking your bare bottom ever since I watched Jonquil turning it a lovely bright red. Sorry, Juicy, but you either go across my knee or I go home. Which is to be?'

As you can imagine, it took no time to make up my mind that a sore bottom was infinitely preferable to the rest of the weekend without Chrissie, so I stood up and waited uneasily for my punishment to get underway, watching as she found a suitable chair, sat down and patted her lap.

Across I went and, after a brief wriggle to get myself balanced and reasonably comfortable, I settled down and tried to compose myself.

'Good girl,' she encouraged gently. 'Now lift up so I can get your jeans down.'

I obeyed, and as I felt her fingers fumbling around the brass button and then the zip, I slowly started to get into it. I still felt it was all wrong to submit to a friend and equal, but the submissive part of my nature was too deeply ingrained to prevent me from getting something of a kick from being spanked – even by Chrissie. Especially as I fully deserved to be punished.

Then I felt her left arm press down on the small of my back, took a deep breath and concentrated on taking it bravely.

She hurt me a lot. At first I thought she was more angry with me than Jonquil had ever been, then that the long gap since my last beating had allowed me to forget how painful it was, then I wondered if a girl's bottom gets soft after a long interval between punishments. But not long after that little thought I gave up all speculation and just tried as hard as I could to keep my bottom reasonably still. I didn't have to worry about making too much noise, and cried out uninhibitedly as my bum got steadily hotter and hotter. Actually, I found it helped, and as Chrissie said nothing about me keeping quiet, I assumed she was quite happy with the evidence that I was suffering.

Another similarity with Jonquil's spankings was that once or twice Chrissie gave us both a little break, during which I could pull myself together and she could have a good feel of my punished flesh. She also pulled my cheeks apart to look at my anus and, much more welcome, commented favourably on the shape and consistency of my buttocks, the depth of my cleft, my pretty folds and, most frequently of all, what a lovely red bottom I had.

And each time my mind tuned even more into the punishment. By the time she started again all my resentment at being spanked by her had disappeared. I began to be genuinely grateful for the way she was dealing with me, realising she had already worked off most of her anger and that I would have hated it if she punished me in any other way.

Not that she was turning me on. My bottom was far too sore for sexual thrills, but I gradually realised I was finding being dominated by her even more exciting than submitting to Jonquil, possibly because I could be reasonably confident that she would comfort me afterwards with an intimacy my erstwhile boss had never seen fit to offer.

And I was absolutely right. When she did eventually stop, and I was limp, exhausted, crying like a baby and very, very sore, she immediately helped up and sat me on her lap, considerately making sure my bottom was clear of both the seat and her thighs. Then she held my head against her shoulder with one hand and stroked my buttocks very gently with the other. After a while my tears dried up, the pain faded to that lovely glow and she brought me to a soft and gentle climax.

After another little cuddle I had to get up, strip naked, stand in front of her so she could admire her handiwork, and then kiss her.

I sensed immediately that I'd been forgiven and that we were back on equal terms. So I made her undress, admired her white bottom, then wanted to compare and contrast, so we went upstairs to my bedroom, which boasted a full length mirror, and stood beside each other, peering over our shoulders at an arresting sight.

Then I dug out my copy of the video and we watched it together. To my immense relief she seemed to enjoy it a lot, and although she'd never seen anything like it before, was bright enough to echo several of the comments made by the more experienced members of the Lenderby's group of friends.

Then we had another shower, and Chrissie spent nearly as long soaping and rinsing my bottom as she had smacking it, and there are no prizes for guessing which I enjoyed more, although I would have reluctantly admitted that the smacking did me a lot more good than the washing.

By the time we finished supper and cleared away I had fully recovered from my punishment, both physically and mentally, and so I was pleased when Chrissie asked if we could watch the video again. For the first time I could actually sit back and enjoy it. Probably because by then I felt enough confidence in my efforts and wasn't anxiously looking for adverse reactions from others.

We both agreed that Susan was amazingly sexy, and I was about to admit that I had her phone number and had every intention of asking her over, but rather unwisely in the event, kept quiet.

By the time the film was over it was dark, just late enough for bed, and we were both very randy indeed.

This time I really enjoyed being in charge of the proceedings. I suppose that subconsciously, I wanted to put my spanking behind me and show her that I was not going to submit to her willy-nilly. It was fine to offer my bottom when I had genuinely offended her, but that was as far as I was prepared to go. Not that Chrissie showed the slightest reluctance to let me ravish her, so I did unto her very much what she had done unto me, not having the experience to follow any different paths, and thoroughly enjoyed myself. Her skin felt especially silky, she smelt absolutely great, her nipples puckered and swelled until they were as hard as little nuts, her sighs, moans, groans and shrieks provided eloquent testimony to her enjoyment and, best of all, I got a real kick from easing the lips of her sex apart and kissing and licking the succulence inside. I'd never done that to a girl before, and realised immediately that I had seriously missed out.

I enjoyed making her come several times, so much that it only took a few seconds of her skilful fingers to do the same for me and we both eventually slept like logs.

If Friday and Saturday had seen a considerable advance in my education, Sunday took it even further. The forecast had been for an improvement throughout the day and, for once, the weather followed suit, with enough blue sky behind the dark clouds to suggest we could have an afternoon in the open air.

After breakfast I went out to get the Sunday papers and asked Chrissie to wash up and clear away. Well, to be honest, I did rather order her to, but lightly enough for her not to feel put down.

I took my time, had a chat to a couple of familiar faces in the shop, drove back slowly through the drizzle, parked, made a dash for the back door and was greeted by an array of dirty dishes. My first reaction was a mixture of annoyance and disappointment but then, in a flash, I felt a surge of unholy glee. I was certain she had done nothing on purpose, probably to test me, and so tested she was going to be – across my knee and with her knickers down.

Suddenly I felt quite breathless. When I watched Jonquil spank her I'd been too preoccupied with my own bottom to feel much more than sympathy, followed by the curiosity that led to the video. And while filming that I'd been too involved with the technicalities to have more than fleeting thoughts about what it would actually be like to spank another girl; the sum of my experience was the two slaps I gave Sharon.

Now the thought of spanking Chrissie for real appealed enormously, so when she ambled in, apparently dressed in nothing more than a T-shirt and sat down with one of the papers, any doubts I may have had about my right to spank her vanished.

I looked pointedly at the piled-up draining board, but

she didn't seem to notice. So I cleared my throat, she looked up, smiled, and went back to the front page.

I took several deep breaths, revelling in what was a very new and exciting experience. I remember quite clearly being a little surprised that the physical sensations of anticipating a spanking were remarkably similar whether one was about to be on the receiving end or dishing it out. My hands were moist and a bit shaky, my knees felt a little weak, and there was that strange hollowness in the pit of my stomach.

I had always assumed that the last was purely down to fear, but as I built up my nerve to tell Chrissie I was about to put her across my knee and smack her, I realised it was more than that. Certainly when Jonquil did it for the first time I was scared, basically of the unknown, but afterwards I had to admit to myself that I found the submission exciting.

I realised I was quite nervous as I gazed in the general direction of the sink. I couldn't be a hundred percent sure that Chrissie would meekly submit her bottom to me, and I certainly wasn't confident enough either to stand my ground in an argument or to be sure I could overcome her by force.

So there was only one thing to do. Take the bull by the horns. I cleared my throat again and broke the silence.

'Sorry, Chrissie, but I really don't expect to have to do everything. I did ask you to clear up and you haven't even apologised for not doing it.'

'Don't worry, Juicy, I'll do it after I've finished with this bit of the paper,' she replied calmly.

The hollow glow intensified. 'Too late,' I announced

quietly but firmly. 'I'm going to spank you. I'm going to do it on your bare bottom and I'm going to do it now. Put the paper down and come into the sitting room.'

She looked at me steadily, her face pale except for a small pink patch on each cheek. Trying to keep any trace of nervousness from my expression, I stared levelly back at her, remembering how Jonquil's air of quiet authority had so impressed me that first time. And on every other occasion!

'I'm sorry, Lucy,' she said after several minutes. 'I should have done it. I'm sorry.'

'Not half as sorry as you will be in about twenty minutes, my girl,' I replied with intense satisfaction, as I took her hand and led her into the sitting room.

I was just too excited. She was wearing a little G-string under her T-shirt, so when I settled her on my lap I was treated to the mouth-watering sight of her lovely cheeks peeping out from under the hem, which had ridden up as she settled into position. I remember that view clearly enough, and how I inched her shirt up very slowly.

We had a bit of a debate about whether to bare her bottom completely, and I suggested that as her buttocks were almost completely bare anyway, her underwear could stay up. She, however, asked me to do the job properly and pull them down.

The memory of the few moments before I started to spank her will stay in my mind for ages, as will the indelible impression left by the first spank – the lovely noise, the way her bottom quivered and rippled, the pink mark, the shift in the weight on my thighs as the impact drove her against me, and then as she wiggled her hips at the flash of pain.

The feel of my stiff palm sinking into her flesh was gorgeous, and her pitiful cries of pain were music to my ears.

But best of all was the heavenly sense of power over her. Not that I had the slightest desire really to hurt her, but I seriously enjoyed registering my disapproval of her laziness, knowing full well that, when it was all over and her bottom had recovered, we'd be back to our usual relationship.

Eventually I looked down on a very red and obviously sore bottom. I nursed my aching palm and studied her quivering cheeks, fascinated by the different blotchy shades. Then I remembered how they'd looked after Jonquil spanked her. The redness had been much more even and I realised I'd not been nearly methodical enough.

I began to stroke her, making suitably soothing noises and, as she got the message that her punishment was over, she, like I had done, burst into tears. I helped her to her feet, turned her round so that she could sit on my knee and held her tight, cupping her hot buttocks in my left hand.

All too soon it was time for Chrissie to head back home, and we kissed each other goodbye. When the echoes of her departure had faded away I went back out to the patio, enjoying the cooling air of a beautiful evening and happy to be alone with my thoughts.

The main one was to thank all the gods anyone had ever believed in for my amazing luck. The fact that Chrissie was such a perfect lover was almost too much to take in, and for that reason alone I was quite glad that we had an enforced break from each other. I needed time to put my mind to other priorities, from making sure the agency didn't forget about me, to settling in and getting to know the village, the people, and that lovely part of England.

Luckily the agency hadn't forgotten me, and Chrissie and I were soon back in harness, working flat out on a difficult pitch for a small chain of supermarkets. They were at the lower end of the scale in terms of both status and size, and therefore presented quite a challenge. We spent a couple of days in London, enduring interminable meetings with the account handling team, the media lot, research and marketing, and then decided to escape to Kent and peace, quiet and no distractions. I suddenly found London a bit too much for longer than about eight hours at a time.

I did have one little worry about my relationship with Chrissie, however. Would the fact that we had spanked and made love to each other affect our ability to create advertising? Luckily, I soon realised the answer was definitely no. We concentrated hard on the campaign, visited several branches of the supermarket in the area, formed clear conclusions, and after a couple of days our ideas had taken shape. Chrissie began to write detailed copy while I drafted out some storyboards.

After a week we took the train back to town, quietly confident that we had found a reasonably attractive and probably effective basis for the campaign. Basically, as the chain didn't score over the competition in terms of the obvious selling points of price and/or quality, we decided to go for subtlety rather than stridency, and our idea for the opening sixty second commercial was a young woman, fairly smartly dressed but not making any obvious statement about herself, stuck in traffic, seeing one of the stores and deciding to do her shopping there. The camera trailed her round, hearing her ask one or two assistants for help, being obviously pleasantly surprised by the range of items available and, when she paid, looking a bit taken aback when the check-out girl checked her money and handed back ten pounds.

With an eye to keeping up the campaign's momentum, we also had our girl bump into a man and exchange tips, with fairly clear hints of mutual attraction. We didn't mind that one of the coffee people had got there first because we were going to be far more subtle about any suggestions of a romance.

Anyway, our ideas were basically approved by Clive and the other directors involved and we had the usual agonising wait, first for the presentation to the client and then, considerably worse, for their decision.

During that time Chrissie used the excuse of a heavy summer cold and fled to the restorative comfort of my cottage in general and my bed in particular, where we carried on much as we had before.

I still hadn't had any inspired ideas for the theme of my next spanking video, and I sensed that Clive and Jonquil were beginning to worry. Nothing was said, but one or two subtle hints on the phone were enough to spur me on.

So Chrissie and I put our heads together, watched the

first one again and tried to go about it with the same professional approach we brought to our advertising projects – objectives, methodology and all that stuff. Before we'd even agreed on the objectives, we suddenly had a fit of giggles and decided the only way was to isolate at least some of the aspects of CP which turned us on, and then look for a basic plot to knit them together.

We began to debate the whole subject, trying to analyse our feelings, either when being punished or when spanking someone else. I revived the argument about whether it was better to take the erring girl's knickers down before starting, or to make it a gradual process.

It seemed a good idea to try it out, and Chrissie put me across her knee, gave me several pretty crisp ones on the seat of my pants, and we were in complete agreement that although there was an extra element of suspense on both sides, the impact of the spanks on both mind and bottom was lessened.

Then she tucked them right up into the groove between my cheeks and spanked me again, which stung as much as it should but still didn't feel quite right.

I then suggested that it was only fair to change places, and had no hesitation in confirming that the cleft is such a key part of a bottom that to have it hidden by rucked-up knickers reduced the impact considerably. As I wanted my videos to be as much about girlish bottoms as punishment for the sake of it, we agreed on bare from the outset.

We then experimented with other approaches to the stripping and, eventually agreed that it was marginally more effective to be bent before being bared, mainly because the feeling of one's last bit of protection being eased over tight buttocks was just that bit more pointed.

We also discussed whether it worse to have your bottom bared for you or to have to do it yourself. We couldn't quite make up our minds and decided that a lot would depend on the circumstances. And we did agree that on the whole, having it done would be more humiliating and doing it yourself more submissive.

It had been fun, our bottoms were pink and tingling nicely, but we hadn't made any progress, so it was clothes back on and separate chairs.

The basic problem was that I wanted to get away from the college scene but neither of us could come up with a convincing alternative. We agreed that a domestic scenario was probably the most realistic – we guessed rather than knew that by far most spankings in the late twentieth century were administered to partners but, from the dramatic point of view, a man beating his submissive girlfriend or wife lacked the element of dramatic surprise which had enlivened my first effort. Apart from anything else, at that stage I was hooked on girl-to-girl action.

For lack of anything better to do, we ran the college film again and I realised that Susan's experience could provide us with just the kick-start we wanted. I dug out her number, got hold of her straight away and, to my delight, discovered not only that she lived less than an hour's drive away, but also that she was completely free and would love to see me again.

My only reservation was an unworthy one. I had sometimes fantasised about having the voluptuous

107

headmistress all to myself, usually with her playing the dominant role, and I would have preferred it if Chrissie had been elsewhere. On the other hand, the thought of watching her being dealt with by Susan had definite appeal – and her reactions to seeing Susan on screen mirrored mine, so I had no doubts that the visit would be a success.

And it was. The only thing that didn't go exactly as planned was that I only saw Chrissie across Susan's knee right at the end, by which time I was so shattered I couldn't really appreciate it. Otherwise, the two of them had me living up to Chrissie's new nickname right from the word go. She started it, of course. When Susan rang through from the gate I pressed the button to open it and went out to welcome her, keenly looking forward not just to seeing her again, but confident that she would be as sexy away from the film set as she had been on it.

She got out of the car, had a quick look round, inhaled the fresh air appreciatively, and then held her arms out in obvious invitation. I stepped forward, expecting the normal kiss on each cheek, but was immediately enveloped in a tight hug and two lovely soft lips were glued to mine.

As I have said, there was something amazingly sexy about her – an air of knowing innocence and a captivating wiggle when she walked. So I was enjoying myself no end, especially when she dropped her hands to the seat of my light summer skirt and began to knead speculatively. We disengaged our mouths, smiled happily and I felt brave enough to reach down for her bottom, which proved to be so round and softly yielding that I could hardly wait to get it naked. Given another couple of minutes I'm sure I would have succeeded, but Chrissie made a very special appearance behind me and that was it.

'Put her down, Juicy, and give the poor girl a chance.' I frowned at her impudence at using my embarrassing nickname in public, remembered that I had threatened her with a spanking if she ever did just that, and was about to announce her imminent fate when Susan forestalled me.

'Why are you…?' Her eyes widened as she caught sight of my friend, and suspecting the worst I whirled round. Sure enough, Chrissie was wearing a pair of espadrilles, a broad grin, and nothing else. I took a deep breath, mentally debated whether it would be best to spank her there and then, or to pretend that nothing out of the ordinary was happening and catch up with her when Susan had gone. But before I could give the matter more than a second's consideration, I was overtaken by events.

'Called Juicy?' Chrissie finished off Susan's question, ginning impishly. 'Because her cunt gets so juicy when it's played with.'

I glared at her, shrugged at Susan who was looking at me speculatively, and desperately tried to get things back to something resembling normality. 'Lovely to see you again, Susan,' I began, my voice only just falling short of a squeak. 'Would you like a coffee? Oh, by the way, this is Chrissie, my friend, colleague and amateur nudist.'

If I had hoped to embarrass Chrissie, I was out of luck. She took the couple of steps required to close the gap between her and our quest, hugged her, kissed her full on the lips and told her she had thoroughly enjoyed her performance on the video and couldn't wait to see her naked for real.

I gaped in disbelief as Susan smiled at the compliment and immediately started to take her clothes off, which, as they consisted of a light dress, bra and knickers, didn't take long. She was facing Chrissie, so I had her back view to admire. Not that I minded, as her bottom was absolutely gorgeous and I stared at it gratefully, while Chrissie presumably did the same to her front.

'Could you turn round so I can see your bottom?' she said.

'Of course,' Susan replied, and in a trice I was staring at those lovely full breasts and neat triangle of golden curls with equal delight.

She then asked Chrissie to turn round, her equally appealing buttocks were admired and then they turned towards me. Bowing to the inevitable and feeling nice and tingly, I reached for the top button of my blouse, which was as far as I got before Susan said something about putting my alleged juiciness to the test, and they pounced.

Before I knew it Chrissie was holding my arms behind my back and Susan had undone my skirt, let it fall to the ground and was crouching down with her face only inches away from my crotch. As if that wasn't embarrassing enough, she whipped my knickers down to my knees and was looking at me with intense interest. It probably would have been better if I'd shut my eyes and thought of other things, but I found the sight of her face mere inches from my dark red curls rather exciting, although when she got even closer and I heard her take a deep sniff, I felt my face burn as I blushed.

I also had to watch when she extended an elegant forefinger and began to probe between my legs, and the sight and the feel of her was enough to make me live up to my newly acquired name.

Then Susan professed a keen desire to see my bottom, so Chrissie twirled me round and, still holding me tight, lifted her right knee so that my bottom was nicely pushed out.

It was poked, prodded, complimented, patted and slapped, and my juices refused to dry up.

Susan said I had far too nice a bottom to stay white and unspanked, so my knickers were taken off and I was made to walk to the house in front of them, my oscillating rear stark naked, tingling furiously with anticipation and feeling as though I was walking on air.

For the first time I really made the connection between pain and pleasure. Susan sat on my chaise longue, I lowered myself onto her lap, immediately appreciating the difference between a clothed and a naked one, presented my bottom invitingly and revelled in every slap and every addition to the stinging pain. Admittedly, the experienced Susan maintained the balance by stroking my reddening buttocks at frequent intervals and, as my spanking progressed, making even more personal invasions, from parting my cheeks to look at my bottom-hole and sex lips, to fingering them and then penetrating both until I had a very nice climax.

I don't know exactly how long it was before we

wearily disentangled ourselves, had a shower, opened a celebratory bottle of champagne and took it out onto the patio outside the sitting room. The one thing I do remember clearly was my introduction to the delicious pleasure of having my bottom-hole licked. I was forced down on my knees with my rump in the air, my cheeks were smacked, and then light slaps to my little orifice sent jarring thrills right up my back passage, irresistibly reminding me of Greg. Then I felt something warm and wet there and the unexpectedly thrilling sensation blew my mind completely. Then I worked out what was touching me there and I straightened up with a squeal of outrage.

Susan, looking deliciously dishevelled, told me not to be a silly girl, slapped my thighs, told me to bend forward again and carried on. Amazed that anyone should actually want to lick me there, I did as I was told. And once I had got over my unease, was forced to admit that it was only just less blissful than the same attentions paid to my clitty.

Then they took it in turns to stick their bottoms out for my tongue, and I was so spaced out by then that I applied it with hardly a qualm.

Another couple of glasses of chilled fizz, enjoyed in a contented silence, restored me and I raised the subject of the video. Susan immediately suggested another one set in the college and modestly offered her services again. I explained why I wanted a change, she accepted that once I'd agreed that I would certainly consider doing another college one at a later date, and we started tossing ideas around.

I then let the other two discuss ideas and thought about it all. It occurred to me that the essential element was that in the normal course of events, none of us were especially dominant. We were pretty equal. Except when it came to sex, when Chrissie definitely took the initiative more than I did. I shied away from the memory of how she and Susan had controlled me right from the beginning, and my thoughts began to crystallise.

'I think I've got it,' I interrupted. They stopped chattering and looked at me, and I was pleased to see that both were giving me their undivided attention with no signs of condescension, proving that they understood my submissiveness was basically confined to sex, not business.

'How about two girls working together,' I continued. 'Alone, in the same office. It's a small company, the boss is away and they have a vital job to finish. A mail shot, for example. One of them makes some sort of mistake, the other has a serious sense of humour failure and the atmosphere gets pretty tense.

'The one who made the mistake is quite a bit older than the other, let's say she's happily married and her husband spanks her regularly. She doesn't admit to actually enjoying it but accepts that it does her a power of good. She confesses this to her colleague, asks her to spank her and, after a bit of persuasion, she agrees.

'Later on, the younger girl also makes a mistake and the tables are turned.'

Chrissie and Susan digested the plot and I was heartened to see growing enthusiasm light up both their faces.

'I like it,' Susan decided after a couple of moments. 'The older one would be sort of directing her own spanking. Asking to have her knickers pulled down, telling her friend to do it a bit harder, that sort of thing. Different, and fun.'

'Yes,' said Chrissie, 'and by using two cameras, you could show how they both react. The younger girl very dubious to start off with but finding the sight of her colleague's bare bum increasingly exciting.'

'And when she's finished spanking her, she would make her carry on working naked from the waist down,' Susan broke in with a glint in her eye. 'I liked the shots in our video, where you showed us walking around with our bottoms bare.

'One thing, though,' she went on. 'I don't see how you can bring in other implements. A cane, or paddle at least. Not convincingly.'

I frowned. I hadn't really given any thought to anything other than a hand spanking, mainly because I'd only had the cane twice and not enjoyed it. Neither had the caning sequences in the first video done much to make me change my opinion. I had gone along with them because everyone else expected me to, but I was much happier to keep my next production to spanking only. Basically, I suppose, because at that stage I found one female smacking another sexy and fulfilling, whereas anything stronger struck me as pure punishment and therefore not really a proper subject for entertainment. But before I could try and explain, Chrissie leapt in.

'I know,' she cried. 'Why not have the boss coming in unexpectedly and catching the two of them, not only way behind schedule but both virtually naked and with red bottoms. He's a real CP enthusiast and we could make the finale a session in his office the following day. Perhaps another little spanking to warm them up and then some with the paddle, and finally a good caning.'

'Brilliant,' was Susan's verdict, and bowing to their greater experience, I agreed. Together we worked out a detailed synopsis, e-mailed it to Clive and Jonquil's flat, persuaded Susan to stay the night and opened another bottle before a late lunch.

Four weeks later I was back in the studio at the office – to edit my second video rather than to let Jonquil have her evil way with my bare bottom. Not that I didn't glance at the spare chair and remember those painful but highly educational sessions, but the absorbing job of putting the considered output from two cameras together kept me occupied for the whole of that Sunday and, far more confident than the first time, I had the finished tape ready to show to Clive and Jonquil by the evening. Part of me was relieved that it was a far more informal viewing than the first one, but I'd be lying if I didn't have the occasional pang of regret that the others weren't there to see the film. Especially Jane – and I wouldn't have minded seeing Roger again, either.

The three of us watched the film in deferential silence, and with me watching their reactions more than the action. At the end they turned to me, nodded and smiled. 'Well done, Lucy,' they said in perfect harmony, and I sat back with a sigh of relief at what was, for them anyway, fulsome praise.

I was pleased with the end result and enjoyed the actual filming much more than the first time, probably because I'd come to terms with the fact that I enjoyed spanking and making films about it. I had been completely uninhibited for one thing. Both the girls selected by Jonquil were both attractive and convincing, and I hadn't hesitated for a moment in getting them to bare their bottoms so I could see what poses suited them best. The girls blushed a bit at first, but soon entered into the spirit of things and were increasingly at ease with their nudity and my interest in it. And Chrissie's for that matter, as she insisted on being there in case she was needed to make any changes to the script.

Greg was in cracking form and his presence did a lot to relax the girls, both of whom were predominantly straight. I was especially pleased with the way they both acted in the lead up to Meryl's spanking. The younger girl, Josie, had a lovely expressive face and Greg and I made sure we captured the way she changed from obviously doubting the point of giving her colleague a good smacking to a growing enthusiasm for the whole idea as she first saw her bottom, then felt it, and after some encouraging, spanked it.

It helped that Meryl had a very nice bottom indeed. She was a striking woman anyway, with lovely brown hair, warm eyes, a laughing mouth and ample curves in all the right places. Her buttocks quivered deliciously when she was spanked and the only downside was that her skin took longer than usual to show the effects. She was definitely into CP and directed her punishment absolutely as scripted, suggesting various changes in her position across Josie's lap to make her bottom look and feel different, as well as crying towards the end, showing it was a genuine and deserved punishment.

Josie was just as good as the dominant one, spanking with growing authority and, when it came to making Meryl take her skirt and knickers off, gave the order with the right mixture of enjoyment and cruelty.

Greg and I took up the same stations we'd used in the first film. He concentrated on the bottoms while I moved from head to side, so that I had plenty of footage of the girls' facial expressions.

One little sequence which worked very well was when Josie forgot to collate the printed mail shots, so that all Meryl's efforts to get the labels done was to no avail and they would end up having to work really late. There was a brief argument while Josie defended her bottom, but Meryl implacably insisted on equal treatment for both and sat down, patting her bare thighs to make her point.

I focused on Josie's nervous face as she looked down at the tempting lap, while Greg filmed the pale thighs and dark, curly bush. As she began to bend down, her face gradually filled my camera while Meryl's thighs filled Greg's. When I edited I used several jump cuts, interposing the face and the thighs to show the naughty girl's reluctant progress as she got into position.

Greg then came up with a touch of genius. We filmed the same sequence twice more, once with me in front, with a full length shot of Josie bending over and Greg behind her catching the tightly filled seat of her slacks changing shape. The second one was from behind Meryl, following her pink bottom as she sat down. I repeated that sequence in slow motion for the final master tape, and the subtle changes in the shape of her bum as she lowered it onto the stool were great. Apart from the visual treat, the build up in tension was marked.

Both spankings were different enough in execution to make for a good degree of variety, on one hand because the two bottoms provided a nice contrast; Meryl's mature cheeks quivered and wobbled beautifully, while Josie's compact little rump afforded us some lovely views of her neat anus and shaven sex. The girls played their parts to perfection, with Meryl understandably more stoic than her young friend, who squealed and pleaded for mercy almost from the start.

Greg and I choreographed the scene leading up to the boss's surprise entrance with special care. I was adamant that, although there was no spanking action and therefore the idea was to give the watcher a breathing space, we should still make sure that we included lots of footage of their naked bottoms as the girls went about their normal tasks. Admittedly I had come to appreciate female bums only recently, but I was convinced that most of the people watching that sort of video would often look at a pretty girl in the street, office or wherever and fantasise what she was like underneath her clothes. Especially bending down to get at the bottom drawer of a filing cabinet. Even I had done that in my last days at Lenderby's.

So we had walking action, in both close-up and full length; bending and squatting, and close-ups of red buttocks being gingerly lowered onto chairs. We also cut in the occasional shot of a face, usually with a slight smile, obviously gazing at the exposed flesh.

The finale, of both girls being beaten, did quite a bit to change my mind on the sexiness of more severe CP. To begin with, I was far more aware of the tension in the air as the girls were sentenced and got ready first for the paddle and then for the cane. I managed to get some of this on film, mainly by focusing on the telltale signs; tongues flickering over dry lips; nervously working fingers; moist palms being dried on thighs. Best of all was when the boss – an actor named Dave – told Josie that the paddle had only been the warm up and that she was going to get a sound caning. I had her startlingly red bottom filling my lens and she instinctively clamped them together at the dire threat. It was far more eloquent than her stuttered protests and pleas to be let off with some more from the paddle.

Both implements excited me. So much so, that when we had shot the last scene – the two naked girls walking slowly back to their office to retrieve their clothes, red-eyed and with beautifully marked rears – I dared to ask Dave to give me a taste of them. He eagerly agreed, so I took down my jeans and knickers in front of everybody and adopted the pose he'd made the girls take up; feet apart and elbows on knees.

I knew exactly how revealing it was and my heart was pounding like my mad as I waited for the first smack – and how it *stung*! The pain seemed to last for an age before fading to a lovely glow, and I really felt my buttocks being flattened by the impact of the thick wood.

The cane was a known quantity, although it felt even

more painful on an already sore bottom.

I only took six with the paddle and three with the cane, but that was more than enough to have me treating Meryl and Josie with real respect for the way they'd taken many more of each.

After we wrapped, Greg and I kissed them all goodbye and began to pack everything up. Realising we were alone, we smiled at each other.

My hands reached for the button of my jeans and, with my heart hammering all over again, I turned my back to him and eased my jeans and knickers down. I thought about taking them right off, but assumed he would prefer to see the object of his desires framed by disarrayed clothing. I knelt down, shuffled my knees as far apart as I could and pushed my bottom out until I could feel cool air on my anus.

I felt a strange exhilaration. My buttocks were still throbbing, although the worst of the pain had faded to a hot glow. I found it hard to understand why I was abasing myself like that, willingly offering the most personal and intimate part of my body to him. For him to do just about the most humiliating thing he could do to me. And after a whole day with me in charge, telling the others what I wanted them to do and making sure that they did it – even Greg.

I knew he was, in a peculiar way, reasserting his status, both as a man and as a better and more experienced director than me. That made it all a bit more understandable, if only marginally less uncomfortable.

I wanted a reminder of the occasion, and turned my head to ask if he had any film left in the camera he used to take some stills for the leaflet promoting the video. I turned as I spoke, and the naked lust in his eyes as he stared at my obscenely displayed bottom made me shudder, then I crouched while he took the photos, after which he put the camera down and knelt behind me.

I began to take deep slow breaths, building myself up for the half-forgotten pain as he prepared to sink his nice big cock into my poor bottom. I felt the pressure against my sphincter and moaned in anticipation.

He eased into me, and instinct made me push back. It helped, and made his initial thrust less painful than I remembered from the first time. But it still hurt. Especially as my buttocks were still pretty sore and the pressure of his hairy belly against them didn't help.

But then the pleasure began to combine with the pain, and gradually I was able to move my bottom in time with his thrusts, to squeeze my anus, making him groan with delight, and that pleased me intensely.

After a while he reached for my clitty. Typically considerate, he tried to make us come together, but I was quite glad that he came first, because when I did his cock had begun to soften a bit, so that the natural spasms of my anus were less uncomfortable.

That time we were not disturbed, so were able to have a bit of a cuddle afterwards, which helped take my mind off my throbbing buttocks and aching back passage.

It was a perfect end to a good day.

Except that it wasn't quite the end. On our drive back home Chrissie noticed me shifting uneasily on my seat and soon wormed the truth out of me. To my relief she wasn't upset with me, and when we got home she announced that I was in for a session of TLC to my bottom. She washed it gently, led me to bed, and then made me kneel while she licked until sweet bliss overcame the ache.

'You're all juicy again,' she whispered huskily, and applied a skilful finger to my cunt as she set to again with her tongue.

It was sheer and absolute heaven!

Chapter Four

The first half-hour of the day was brilliant. Chrissie had already left to catch the early train to London, where she had to be at a client presentation that didn't involve me. I had the day completely to myself, and it showed every sign of living up to the good weather forecast. We had both been working pretty hard on the creative proposals and I was seriously looking forward to chilling out.

It was a month or so after the completion of my second spanking video, so I was thinking about the next one, after a reasonable amount of ordinary advertising work for Lenderby's. I was working quite hard, enjoying it and making enough money to have no real worries, helped by a totally unexpected cheque from Clive, which he explained was my share for the sales of *College Tails*, the first video. Apparently, he and a couple of other members of his group of friends actually distributed the videos, with a high percentage going to the continent and the beginnings of a breakthrough into the States in the offing, so I knew I would get a fair deal in the future. In the meantime my fee for *Office Tails* was safely in my deposit account, with the promise of more from royalties.

Even more important, Chrissie and I were really settling down together. After a couple of weeks of her coming down only at weekends, she had taken it on herself to have a quiet word with Clive, after which he agreed to put her on the same freelance basis as me, and also suggested that she could act as my assistant on the spanking videos and earn extra that way.

She broke the news to me one Friday evening. I successfully disguised my happiness at her desire to move in with me on a more permanent basis, and sentenced her to a sound spanking for not having the decency to discuss it with me first.

All in all, Chrissie was turning out to be a little jewel. It helped a lot that she was strikingly attractive, but all her other qualities were just as important. As I said earlier, that sweet exterior hid the machiavellian heart of an enthusiastic slut. Unlike any boyfriend I'd ever had, she enjoyed non-sexual contact. One rather chilly noon, after we'd spent all morning stuck in our little office, we agreed that a picnic in the woods would clear our heads. It was jeans and sweaters weather, and half an hour just lying in each other's arms, talking desultorily and feeling as close mentally as we were physically.

We were invited to a couple of local parties, and to my immense relief she not only behaved herself but was such fun that our social life began to take off. When she first stayed with me I was a little diffident about introducing her to my local acquaintants, mostly at the local pub, as I wasn't sure how country people would react if they suspected our sexual inclinations. But in the event they either didn't suspect or didn't care. The strict churchgoers would probably have at least raised the odd eyebrow, but I tended not to gravitate towards that section of the community in any case, so was hardly likely to lose much sleep over their opinions.

It helped that Chrissie was a dreadful flirt at the best of times, and the way she fluttered her eyelashes at one charming retired colonel had the old boy glowing with pleasure, and his very nice wife looking at him with a combination of resignation and pride. I came away from that party feeling that any rumours would probably be quashed with military efficiency.

Chrissie and I had quickly worked out that CP was easily the best way to settle our occasional differences, and as she was just as careless as I was, her bottom came in for its fair share.

It isn't as though spanking dominated our lives. It was undoubtedly a key element in what was a rich and colourful tapestry, but our work, the lovely countryside around us, the village and its people all provided pleasure and contentment.

The local pub gradually became the centre of our social life. I had been a little worried that old-fashioned attitudes to women in what had traditionally been bastions of male gatherings would still prevail and we would only be tolerated rather than made really welcome, but I was wrong.

It was, apart from anything else, a lovely old building, run by a very nice couple who were themselves enthusiastic participants in village life. Both they and their bar staff had the knack of being interested in their customers without crossing the fine line into nosiness. The food was excellent and we soon made a few genuine friends and a lot of nice acquaintances.

We were offered horses to ride, but I said I'd come to an arrangement with horses; if I didn't get on their backs, they wouldn't throw me off, and it was all working to the satisfaction of both parties. My excuse was received with smiling acceptance, not snobbish contempt.

Being a good player, Chrissie was soon a popular member of the tennis circle and I went along to watch whenever I could. Apart from the intense pleasure of watching others running years off their lives, she looked utterly adorable in her little white T-shirt and skirt. And she was good enough to make me begin to enjoy a game I had never paid any attention to before.

As the weeks drifted by, however, I found I occasionally lost that priceless feeling of quiet contentment that is so much more rare than happiness. Every now and then I found myself jogging harder and further than I was used to and, judging from the aches and pains later, more than was good for me.

Even though I was getting to care for her more and more, I would find myself snapping at her for no good reason. She may well have been able to get rid of any hurt and irritation by thrashing my bare bottom, but it was not a good thing as far as our relationship was concerned, although we usually made up with a kiss and a cuddle.

When we got an e-mail from Jonquil asking us to dinner and offering us a bed for the night, I leapt at the invitation with more enthusiasm than Chrissie, sensing there was something unusual in the offing.

When we arrived I again took in the perfection of the sitting room, the stunning view of the Thames, and lastly the gathered people. I was a little disappointed that Clive wasn't there, pleased to recognise the nice lady doctor, Jane, who'd been at the first showing of *College Tails*, and rather perturbed to see Morganna, the enigmatic woman who'd also been there.

I smiled at them both, accepted a welcoming kiss from Jonquil, who was looking even more ravishing than ever, a glass of champagne, and then moved to an armchair and sat down, avoiding the empty space on the sofa next to Morganna.

We had a few glasses to drink, during which the conversation got much less stilted, and then moved into the dining room for one of Jonquil's typically exquisite feasts.

Not surprisingly, the talk soon turned to the subject most dear to the hearts of all present – the female body in general and the bottom in particular. Apart from the fact that I was more than happy with the conversational direction, I was again pleasantly surprised at the completely open way everybody brought their essentially private thoughts and enthusiasms into the open, knowing they would not cause either mockery or embarrassment.

At that stage I felt much less experienced than the others, and so tended to listen more than contribute, but even Morganna paid attention to my occasional comments with due respect, and when she differed, expressed her thoughts without even hinting at a put down.

It was after dinner that things got a bit more personal. We were sitting over coffee and the sort of chocolates that add an inch to your hips even if you only smell the wrappers, when Jonquil suddenly asked what I liked best about Chrissie's body.

'Her bottom,' I said straightaway, smiling at the owner, who looked suitably pleased.

'What do you like best about it?' demanded Morganna.

I blinked and tried to kick my relaxed brain into action. 'It – it's so round,' I stammered, wishing I had Chrissie's facility with words, 'and looks so nice and firm until you touch it. Or smack it. Then it's all soft and pliable; girlish and lovely.' I looked round at my audience, all of whom were smiling with what I hoped was sympathetic understanding. I took a deep breath, a gulp of brandy, summoned up several images of my bare girlfriend going about her normal business, then some other far more private memories, and carried on.

I mentioned her tight cleft, and I described what fun it was to seize the opportunity when she wore her leather trousers, and to follow up the stairs to the bedroom, my eyes glued to the shifting flesh so clearly discernible beneath that flexible hide, then to ease them down and kiss the cheeks of her bottom, swelling so nicely from the thong she always wore. The combined scent of a clean and excited Chrissie and leather *really* turned me on.

I also told them how much I loved the rest of her, from her firm thighs and toned tummy, to her lovely breasts with nipples that puckered and stiffened at the slightest stimulation. After I told them all about her succulent sex, with its neat bush and tight slit, I was squirming on my seat and horribly aware that my knickers were very wet indeed, and was half relieved and half disappointed when Jonquil suggested we went back into the sitting room. Although I had quite enjoyed making Chrissie the centre of sexual attention for once, I had a horrid feeling that she was on the verge of turning the tables.

Then, as we were standing by one of the windows absorbing the view of the Thames, I started chatting to Jane. 'Are you in general practice?' I asked.

'No, I'm a consultant surgeon,' she replied, rather guardedly, I thought.

'Oh, do you specialise?'

'Yes… I'm a proctologist.'

Our eyes met and I suddenly remembered what a proctologist does. 'Oh, a bottom doctor?' I said, rather pleased with myself.

'That's right,' she replied unemotionally.

I looked at her seriously and simply spoke my immediate thoughts, bolstered I'm sure by the combination of the relaxed atmosphere and a little too much to drink. 'I was just thinking,' I said slowly, 'that if I were in your shoes and you were my patient, I would probably find it rather difficult to maintain an air of professional detachment. I mean, the thought that I would soon be seeing your bottom all bare would be so exciting I'm sure I'd give myself away.'

She smiled, and it struck me that she really was very attractive indeed, but in such an understated way that it took a bit of time to realise it. Especially with the exotic and rather terrifyingly beautiful Morganna, the simply lovely Jonquil and my stunningly pretty Chrissie as competition.

129

'Thank you,' she said, 'but then you haven't had all my years of training and experience.'

I was beginning to feel a bit stirred by the conversation, even though my basic instinct was to avoid medical situations whenever possible. 'I appreciate that, but don't you sometimes get a patient who attracts you?'

'Of course, but I don't think about that until afterwards.' And then there was a twinkle in her eye as she asked me straight out if I would play the part of a patient for her. 'To be perfectly honest, Lucy, I do occasionally fantasise about… how can I put it…? Really indulging myself, especially with a pretty girl. And you've got such a gorgeous bottom… would you do it for me?'

How could I possibly refuse? 'And would you like to make a private video of it?' I asked with sudden inspiration.

'Oh yes,' she breathed, and I was committed, and didn't have second thoughts until several days later.

After a couple more brandies I was even less capable of resisting Morganna when, having heard about my arrangement with Jane, she asked me to do a similar exercise to demonstrate her 'private little room'.

I had second, third and fourth thoughts about the wisdom of letting myself fall into her clutches, but by that time it was far too late.

The evening ended as I expected; I received a spanking, but when the time came I had come down from my previous high and really didn't feel like being spanked at all. Not that Jonquil, Morganna or Jane even bothered to ask me how I felt about offering my bottom for their amusement. They wanted it so they went ahead and helped themselves.

It helped that Chrissie was also dealt with and went first. By the time it was my turn, the alluring sight of her bare bottom as it wriggled and reddened on Jonquil's lap excited me no end, so I took her place reasonably happily.

I was a bit put out when both Jane and Morganna wanted a crack at us as well. My bottom was quite sore enough after Jonquil's attentions but again, watching while Chrissie took it was quite exciting, and I went over their laps with my interest in firsthand experience of other spanking techniques aroused. I was not surprised that Jane showed as much interest in our bottom-holes as she did our buttocks, and I openly admitted afterwards that I had got pretty wet at the frequent parting of my sore cheeks. Morganna was equally predictable. She spanked hard and very effectively, but when I realised I was getting strange but distinct pleasure from the pain, I relaxed a little.

The following morning was dedicated to agency matters. Jonquil reminded us of a recent article in the trade press in which a respected advertising man had analysed the performance and ethos of a number of agencies, including Lenderby's. On the whole, we had come out of it well, with Chrissie and I mentioned by name as mainly responsible for our recent successful pitches, and praising our commercials for selling the product rather than the agency – which was nice.

On the other hand, the three of us agreed that it would be nice to have the chance to let our creative hair down and have a crack at a product which would respond well to a really way-out campaign. Jonquil asked us to keep our eyes and ears open, and if we saw any product or service advertised and thought we could do better, work up some ideas and she and Clive would try and take it from there. We agreed it wasn't strictly ethical, but that all was fair in love, war and business.

And so, with my sessions with Jane and Morganna to worry about, a spanking video plot to get clear in my mind, and the speculative advertising ideas to think about, my restlessness was less of a worry and Chrissie and I enjoyed a fortnight of peace and harmony.

We shot lots of video, some for our eyes only, some forming a sort of diary of our lives and surroundings, and I soon got the hang of the digital still camera. Chrissie was a perfect model. She was confident enough in her own beauty to pose in the nude without a trace of self-consciousness, but without ever flaunting herself.

Looking at the growing portfolio was a source of pleasure and inspiration. The quality of those I printed out to put up on the walls weren't up to traditional photographic standard, but not at all bad.

We also recorded the state of our bottoms after each punishment, which were getting more frequent and strenuous as both of us grew steadily hooked on the peculiar pleasure of pain. Even fairly minor aggravations resulted in a prolonged session across the other's lap.

As far as I was concerned, I still got the most satisfying kicks from spanking. I was beginning to appreciate more severe treatment, and every now and then I eyed Chrissie's bottom and inwardly assessed whether I dared sentence it and her to a caning.

But nothing was quite like being put across her knee, feeling my knickers slithering down over my buttocks and thighs, lying meekly while she enjoyed a good feel, my bottom tingling in its naked vulnerability, relaxing when she parted my cheeks to inspect my anus and then revelling in the familiar but addictive sounds, wobbles and sting as her hand reddened me appropriately. I had learnt to absorb the pain, to ride it, to revel in the challenge and to love the aftermath. Especially that heady moment immediately afterwards, when I clambered to my feet, half crying with pain, half laughing with relief that it wasn't going to get any worse, rubbing my blazing bottom and looking down at Chrissie, who usually had her hand or the hairbrush to her mouth, kissing the surface which had punished my naked skin so effectively, her face soft with forgiveness and satisfaction at a job well done – and thoroughly enjoyed.

But none of this was much comfort as the time for my session with Jane approached. And even less comforting was the prospect of Morganna waiting in the wings.

I began to have restless dreams, usually involving me being led naked to be beaten in front of a gloating crowd of men and women. I always woke up before the first lash of the unseen implement landed on my carefully positioned bottom, but in some ways that made the dreams worse.

Greg came to stay, and brought a video of an American soft porn film, with one quite exciting scene. One of the actresses was playing the role of an early puritan settler and was sentenced to a whipping. She was led to a pillory, her head and wrists fastened, her dress pulled right down and a nasty looking whip applied forcefully across her bare bottom. Using my video's slow motion facility, we could see the marks on her skin as the whip landed. We agreed that although it had been pretty sexy, the girl's position was all wrong; kneeling on the ground so that only the upper part of her bottom was accessible, and it would have been much better if her back had been parallel to the ground and her rump thrust in the air; a better target and much more humiliating.

That night I dreamt that I was being dragged to a pillory, one with a block to kneel on, roughly the same height as the pillory and so my cowering buttocks were horribly exposed. In my dream there were dozens of people watching my punishment, all leering horribly and revelling in my plight.

Morganna, dressed in a black leather catsuit, was practising with a vicious whip in front of me, so I could see and hear the sound and fury as she lashed it into a tree, but just then I woke up whimpering and sweating.

Greg came back the following weekend, proudly showing off the pillory he had knocked up in his garage. He dug a hole for it by the side of the house and, as Chrissie and I admired it, he fetched a padded block, very like the one in my dream. I went pale and cold, but we just had to try it out, so I walked up to it with icy fingers playing up and down my spine.

Once the upper part of the hinged top had been locked into place, trapping my head and hands securely, I felt dreadfully helpless. They bared my bottom and spanked me, and all I could do was wriggle and cry out. Greg pointed out that in the old days the miscreant would probably have been standing up and the whipping would have been on the back more than the buttocks. He also told me to be grateful he'd lined the wrist and neck holes with foam rubber for comfort, so I thanked him.

Mind you, I was much more enthusiastic when we put Chrissie in and spanked her bare bottom as soundly as mine had been. That was fun, and I knew I was getting close to a scenario for my next video, but there was Jane and Morganna to deal with first.

We set off for Jane's private surgery in Harley Street on the appointed day, and the journey was not the happiest I've had. My main concern was that I hated hospitals, needles, the smell of whatever it is all medical establishments seem to smell of, and began to doubt that I'd get much from the visit.

Jane greeted us looking very professional in her white coat and stethoscope, and my doubts at the wisdom of allowing myself to be poked and prodded returned in force. Chrissie, by contrast, was vibrating with suppressed excitement, so that we slipped easily into different roles which, as was soon clear, suited Jane down to the ground. I was the nervous little ninny, who didn't want to strip completely naked for the examination, whereas Chrissie couldn't wait to parade her charms.

Not surprisingly, Jane pretended to get irritated with my stupid modesty and put me across her knee, pulled my knickers down and spanked me very hard indeed, while my gloating girlfriend captured every spank, grimace and cry on video.

But when I tearfully undressed, something happened which did surprise me. Jonquil appeared, in a nurse's outfit that was more realistic than fanciful, but still made her look good enough to cause erectile mayhem in any men's ward, and to my complete amazement Jane ticked her off for being late and then spanked her. That was the beginning of the end of my worries. I had never seen her bottom before, and to be quite honest, had never harboured any great desire to. Not because I thought there would be anything wrong with it, but as my professional superior, happily married and my first dominant, she was basically too far out of reach.

As it was, her bottom proved to be as gorgeous as the rest of her, and once I got over the shock, I watched her spanking very happily indeed.

After that Jane claimed she was too hot, took off her coat and revealed everything she wore underneath. Then Jonquil had to tuck her skirt into her belt and remove her knickers, so we could all look at her red buttocks whenever we wanted.

To be quite honest, I would have preferred to sit quietly looking at them to what I went through, even though by the end I was intensely excited.

As I expected, Chrissie and I were put through the medical mill. Out temperatures were taken with a rectal thermometer whilst lying on the examination couch, naked, with everyone staring at my red cheeks and the glass tube poking up obscenely from between them. Having said that, Chrissie did look rather sweet when it was her turn.

We were given a thorough check up, and then the real business started. If having my temperature taken in my bottom had been a bit discomforting, crouching with my rump in the air while Jane stuck first her finger then a rather uncomfortable viewing instrument into my depths was a lot worse. The one thing she did to us which gave some pleasure was an enema. The tube was a lot easier to take than the thingmescope and the relief afterwards was so fantastic I didn't care that they all watched me sitting on the loo.

And again, watching Chrissie pose her lovely bottom so that her sweet little anus was fully exposed, and then see the tube slide into her back passage made my embarrassment worthwhile.

At the end of the visit we drove home, with me delighted to have seen Jonquil's lovely bottom, and another element in the major video taking form in my subconscious.

But before I could get it all together, I had my session with the cruel Morganna to face, and as the time approached I began to get seriously apprehensive about the prospect. Wisely, I decided to go up to London by train, feeling fairly sure that I wouldn't be in a fit state for a longish drive back through London traffic.

The strange thing was that although I knew Morganna was going to torment me far more than Jane had done, I wasn't dreading my session with her nearly so much, probably because the sexual element in her desires was much more obvious than Jane's. And I was by then more at ease with the pain/pleasure equation.

In the event, my first caning from Chrissie probably caused me more actual pain than Morganna did in the couple of hours or so I spent in her clutches. The difference was that Chrissie was beating me on my bare bottom for being careless and inconsiderate, whereas Morganna simply enjoyed hurting me and, arguably even more, degrading me, from the very moment we arrived in her basement, which had been lovingly fitted out as a sort of torture chamber, with racks of implements on every wall, bars set in the floor and against one of the walls, a thing like a padded gym horse and a low long bench.

She started off by making me strip completely naked, then I had to stand, hands on head, feet apart, while she walked slowly round me several times, firstly just looking, then touching.

She then made me watch while she teased my nipples into prominence, and then tightened beautiful jewelled clamps on each one. The pain was initially enough to make me grit my teeth, but soon ebbed away to tolerable levels. Then my sex lips were held open and my clit treated in the same way as my nipples, and the pain was intense.

She connected the three clamps with a delicate chain and adjusted it carefully, so that the level of pain rose just enough to have my breath hissing through my clenched teeth. Then six explosive strokes with a leather paddle made my buttocks shudder and quake. The first made me jerk and the sharp stabs from the clamps reminded me cruelly that I would be well advised to stay still.

With a scorched bottom I offered no protests as she then spent a leisurely ten minutes putting me in a complex apparatus, consisting of a bar to hold my feet wide apart and another for my wrists, which was linked by strong chains to two broad leather slings supporting my thighs. The bar on my wrists was fixed to another strong chain leading to a pulley on the ceiling.

The end result was that I was suspended, my back more or less straight, my knees wide apart and pulled up to a level just below my breasts. It wasn't as uncomfortable as it sounds, as the slings took a great deal of my weight and Morganna had removed the clamps, but it did make my exposure seem all the worse.

'Do you like my clever toy?' she asked.

'Yes, Morganna,' I lied.

'You will call me mistress.'

'Yes, mistress.'

The tone of the session was set and I knew exactly where I stood. I was just a body. One that Morganna evidently desired, as the lustful glint in her eyes left me in no doubt.

She put me in all sorts of revealing positions, slowly and inexorably increased the levels of discomfort, and I was only really aware of my aching limbs and utter helplessness.

I was bent over, doubled up, hung up to the ceiling so that only my toes relieved the pressure on my arms, and every so often, to my immense gratitude, strapped to one of the benches where I could at least relax a little.

Then I had to sit on a stool – a very special stool; it had a remarkably lifelike erection spearing up from the seat. With wide eyes I watched her smear lubricant over the obscene length, and my stomach knotted with apprehension. It looked a lot thicker than Greg's, if not as long. Then following her order, I took a deep breath, and with her hands pressing on my shoulders, sank down, impaling my bottom, groaning through the gag that filled my mouth. The cruel woman then compounded my misery by tying my feet to a ring set in the floor, stretching my legs out so that I had to rest my whole weight on the dildo.

Then she tied my hands to the legs of the stool behind me, and at first I had no idea what she intended, but as soon as I saw her eyeing my vulnerable breasts with hungry intent, I knew, and with a breathless mixture of consternation and intrigue, I closed my eyes and waited for the experience to begin.

But Morganna made me watch as the leather strap swept remorselessly down, making my breasts quake every time it bit and steadily turning them from white to pink to red.

It hurt, but nothing compared with the final torment. To be fair she did ask if I was up to six with a sjambok, and my curiosity overcame my doubts, despite being in a bit of a daze, the beating producing an inner glow I had never experienced until then.

She strung me up from the ceiling again, with my parted feet resting flat on the floor. My buttocks felt a little numb as she gently stroked them, and I felt myself slipping into a sensual reverie until a line of scorching agony seared across my tenderised bottom. Amazingly, for several moments after it landed the pain seemed to get more intense, then at last that lovely glow permeated my middle and I hung limply from my wrists, knowing I would not ask to be let off the full six.

When Morganna finally untied me I could hardly stand, but there wasn't a tear in my eyes. Morganna was gentle with me, soothing my marks with a blissfully cool ointment and holding me in her arms until I got my strength back. Then she asked me to lick her bottom. She didn't order me to. She even said please.

Her buttocks were firm, smooth and lovely, and I parted them without a qualm, gazing at her little rear entrance with delight before applying my mouth. I knew she had taken me past a barrier, and that I was much better equipped for the way of life Jonquil had instigated.

Chapter Five

The plot for my next and most complex spanking video finally slotted into place one hot afternoon. Chrissie had decided that all the money she was saving by living with me was gathering dust in the bank and would be far happier in the hands of selected clothes shops. Not feeling like tramping the length of Oxford Street, I let her go on her own, glad to have the chance to be alone. I opened a bottle of wine and got to work, and two hours later I had the basic plot neatly written out and the main scenarios on five storyboards. With a satisfied sigh I had lunch and finished the wine, revelling in the peace and quiet on my patio. I was comfortable, the temperature was perfect, and there was enough in the way of background noise from the birds to stop me feeling lonely. I dozed, and my contentment grew.

And I felt even better about life after I'd made the video, which I still consider one of the best I have ever done. Apart from anything else, I decided I would play the leading role. Susan had inspired the thought when she told me she acted in spanking videos for the kicks, not the money, as having her bottom filmed whilst being beaten added something rather special to the occasion.

And so, when Chrissie got back that evening, I showed her my plans and she greeted them with encouraging enthusiasm, and she thought my idea to be in it was a splendid idea. The following day Clive and Jonquil also approved.

And so the scene was set. Greg came down for a briefing, the two of us taught Chrissie some of the finer points of filming and, all too soon, a nervously excited Juicy Lucy was on the way to stardom – or so I hoped. Not that I wanted to be recognised in the street, of course, so I made full use of a theatrical make-up artist friend of Jonquil's to make sure I looked different enough to preserve my real identity.

My vivid dreams provided the main inspiration for the plot, which consisted of a girl – little me – dreaming that her various sins and failings were punished with increasing elaboration and severity by two ominous figures who appeared in her sleep and led her helplessly to her fate. Clive and Jonquil played the two 'ghosts', both dressed in dark full length robes and with large hoods that kept the details of their faces in shadow but, with Greg's lighting skills, we were able to show frequent glimpses of flashing eyes and cruel mouths, especially when they pronounced sentence.

Because I was subjected to five punishments in all, and each one administered to an unmarked bottom, it was quite a complicated shooting script for this type of production and the whole thing took a couple of weeks, even though we used the cottage for all the locations, which saved time. And it was worth it in the end.

The opening shot was of me getting ready for bed. The camera followed me up the stairs and into my bedroom. I was wearing an ordinary skirt, nothing too revealing. In the bedroom I undressed, went naked to

143

the bathroom and stepped into the shower for some nice close-ups of my rear with streams of water flowing over my buttocks. I washed myself, turned slowly to rinse off, then dried myself with a large towel, cleaned my teeth and the camera zoomed slowly in until the lens was filled with my bare bottom, trembling gently as I scrubbed away.

Then back to the bedroom, the camera following closely.

I put on a pair of clingy pyjamas, climbed into bed and turned out the light.

We faded out, and then in to the ghosts slipping quietly into the room. The lights came back up and I sat up blinking, mildly annoyed at the interruption to my beauty sleep rather than frightened.

I was told my house was a tip, that I'd had any number of warnings and that I'd now got to be punished. Their voices were slightly unnatural, with a hollowness to them, and I immediately apologised for my slackness and begged for another chance.

'Too late, my girl,' Clive intoned, took my arm, pulled me out of bed, across to a handily placed chair, put me across his knee, carefully adjusted the seat of my pyjamas so that every curve of my writhing bottom was revealed and began to spank me, methodically and crisply, and I sobbed in protest that I was twenty-three and too old to have my bottom smacked like a child.

'You've behaved like a child and so you'll be treated as a child,' Jonquil said uncompromisingly. Then two more spanks landed and she spoke again. 'She doesn't seem to be feeling it, master. May I suggest…'

'Oh, but I am!' I wailed. 'My bottom's really sore.'

'…that you pull down her pyjama bottoms and do it on her bare bottom,' she continued with unruffled ruthlessness.

My outraged protests were rightly ignored, my pink bottom bared with sensual deliberation and the spanking continued, seen from a variety of angles. Once he'd turned my bottom a rich dark pink, he pushed me back onto my feet, stood up, Jonquil took his place and back down I went, protesting volubly but obviously having decided it would be futile to resist. By the end my buttocks and the tops of my thighs were dark red and I was sobbing helplessly.

Then Clive introduced a new twist. After covering every inch of my bottom, he told me I was going to get six stingers and made me bend my elbows and bring my feet up, lifting my middle even more provocatively.

'Three on each buttock,' he announced, and stingers he said and stingers they were. Each one made me cry out.

After being spanked by Jonquil, I was allowed to get up and told to stand in the corner with my hands on my head, which was a cue for a lingering close-up of my twitching red bottom, then my pyjamas slithering down to my feet. My bottom was adjudged to be pretty red, but not quite red enough, so I was told to kneel up on the sofa and present it for more. I looked at them forlornly, realised there was no point in arguing, then shuffled over to the appointed place. My position was then adjusted until my buttocks were nicely exposed.

The spanking resumed, first with a hand and then a

slipper, which made a dramatic sound as it landed, added significantly to the redness and made my taut cheeks quiver. After careful examination my bottom was deemed to be a beautiful colour and properly punished.

Back into the corner I was sent, another close-up, I was told I could rub it and we faded out as my hands soothed my afflicted rump. We then faded in to me waking up in the morning, remembering my dream and hopping out of bed, over to the mirror and lowering my pyjamas to reveal a pure white bum.

In scene two I was getting into bed, this time in a nightie short enough to show the cheeks of my bottom peeping from below the hem.

My tormentors appeared as before and announced that my behaviour was still slovenly, and I was again behaving like an idle schoolgirl. My face crumpled into a sulky pout and I asked if that meant another spanking.

'Something like that,' Jonquil said dryly, and told me to get out of bed, and they led me along the landing.

We then faded in to me dressed in gym kit, nervously waiting outside a door. There was a notice screwed to it that read *Headmistress*. There was another girl with me; a gorgeous little brunette we'd auditioned named Sally. Looking really uneasy, she turned to me. 'We won't get spanked, will we?' she asked in hushed tones.

'I hope not,' I replied, more in hope than expectation, and then knocked on the door.

'Come!' called Susan from within, in her accustomed role as headmistress, so we crept in and prepared to meet our fate, which turned out to be a hand spanking, then a hairbrush and finally a caning.

Sally was spanked first, and her expression as she walked across to a seated Susan was a picture of anxiety. She was made to stand in front of the headmistress while her short skirt was tucked in at the waist, turning as ordered so that back and front could be dealt with properly.

We filmed from every angle as she followed Susan's continuing instructions and sulkily bent and stepped out of her panties. Her sex was especially inviting, and her bottom was different to mine – slim and tight.

Susan lectured her briefly, while the camera lingered on a close-up of her bare bottom, with Susan's hand wandering purposefully over both cheeks, testing the quality of her flesh, her red fingernails strongly hinting at the colour she planned to bring to those nice little buttocks in the very near future.

Then she put the girl across her knee, assessed the different feel of her upthrust bottom, and then got her spanking underway.

It wasn't a particularly hard spanking but real enough to be exciting to watch. The cameras moved smoothly around, capturing the action from different points of view but always with her bottom in view somewhere. Even when her grimacing face was the centre of attraction, the upper slopes were visible in the background.

When she had been nicely warmed up it was my turn, so Sally moved clear and carefully began to pull her panties up.

'Did I say you could cover yourself, girl?' Susan thundered.

'Um, no, miss,' Sally stammered.

While I watched forlornly, poor Sally had to touch her toes for six blistering spanks. She straightened up and had the presence of mind to ask permission to rub her bottom. This was given, and Susan and I watched her busy hands and shifting flesh with very different expressions – hers of satisfaction, mine of trepidation.

Then it was my turn to be bared and spanked. As I squirmed across Susan's lap I complained softly and continually that she spanked me too hard, that my poor bottom was agonisingly sore, but Susan took not a blind bit of notice.

After three or four minutes she judged my bottom to be red enough and told me to stand up, and Sally had to kneel up on a stool with her bottom presented for six of the best on each buttock with a vicious looking wooden hairbrush. Each resounding stroke had her howling pitifully, and her scarlet buttocks churned and heaved in agony.

Periodic shots of my face showed me pale and drawn, wincing at the sound and sight of my friend's naked flesh being chastised, and occasional shots of my pink bottom showed it clenching with sympathy.

Sally's dozen were administered and she clambered off the stool, sobbing and gingerly clutching her bottom. I took her place and seemed naturally reluctant to present my bottom as vulnerably as Susan wanted, but she lost her temper, nudged my knees apart and pushed my shoulders down.

I started crying, and the first spank swept cruelly into my taut flesh, making me howl. Susan changed her approach and whacked my left buttock six times in succession, and then she and Sally looked at the result and smiled at each other.

The right buttock was then toned up to match and I struggle wearily to my feet, casting a bitter look in the direction of my ghostly tormentors, who had been watching the punishments with evident approval.

Following more orders from Susan, Sally then bent over to touch her toes for six with the cane, which duly landed with envious precision right across her tight little cheeks and made her buck and howl every time. One camera lingered on the contortions of her bottom as she reacted to the pain and then reluctantly offered it up again for the next stroke, while the other focussed on her flushed, tearstained face.

I followed in her footsteps and, unlike her, couldn't resist clutching my poor bottom after each stroke. My frenzied rubs distorted my cheeks, opening the cleft, treating the watchers to several glimpses of my shadowy valley. Susan lost her patience and made me stand upright for two crisp extra strokes across the front of my thighs, and they stung like hell!

After I'd had my bottom caned, Susan made us stand side by side so she could inspect her handiwork at leisure, and then pulled up our knickers, making us both wince uncomfortably, lowered our skirts and dismissed us.

The film then faded to my hands smoothing cold cream into Sally's marked bottom, then hers doing the same to mine, and faded out.

We then finished with me waking up and again looking at my punished rear in the mirror with a puzzled expression on my face, and cut to a final close-up of my bottom as I walked naked to the bathroom.

After a suitable interval we were ready for scene three. We started it as I was getting ready for bed again, this time naked and sitting at my dressing table removing my make-up. I got into bed, put the bedside light out and did my impression of someone asleep.

The ghosts appeared again and woke me up. This time I was nervous rather than frightened, and when they told me I was a rude and unhelpful girl, I pulled a rueful face and admitted that I had at times been thoughtless, to say the least. I asked if I had to be beaten without any obvious hope that the answer would be in the negative, and as I spoke, climbed resignedly out of bed and waited meekly for them to lead me off for punishment.

The camera followed my bare bottom as I was led out of the bedroom and we faded into another shot of it, this time in really tight jeans. Someone was giving me a severe ticking off and my buttocks clenched nervously as the inevitability of punishment dawned on me. We then zoomed out to bring my tormentor into shot.

She was a curvy, blue-eyed blonde, dressed in tight khaki trousers and a khaki shirt with an unidentifiable badge on her left breast, suggesting some sort of policewoman or warden, but without being specific. After a short but terse lecture I was sentenced to a beating.

Zooming out a bit further and we were in a very basic office, with only a desk and a couple of chairs for furniture.

Betsy, the gorgeous blonde, made the most of baring my bottom, feeling the seat of my jeans, tugging them down slowly, having another good feel and then peeling down my knickers.

'You know,' she purred, 'you've got a really cute ass. Round... slightly plump... and deliciously firm. Did you know that?'

'No, ma'am,' I replied. 'Thank you, ma'am.'

'And I bet it'll look even nicer all bare,' she went on with her lines. 'Well, let's have a little feel... mmmm, very nice. All soft and smooth, like a baby's bottom. Oh yes, nice and white too.

'Now, I think the paddle will do nicely for starters. Lean on the edge of the desk, and stick your ass out a little more. That's a good girl. Brace yourself... no, keep those cheeks nice and relaxed. I want to see them wobble when I hit them. That's right, just like that.'

'*Owww*,' I sighed as she struck me for the first time, using precise wristy flicks with an authentic wooden paddle, shaped a bit like a short cricket bat, although thinner and beautifully polished.

The sting was initially breathtaking but faded quickly, and I could sense it wasn't damaging my flesh – just making it hotter and hotter.

She concentrated on my left buttock, leaving the right one alone. It felt peculiar and I was soon at the point of begging her to change sides. She did, and it wasn't too long before I was dying for her to go back to the original one.

Then she made me rest my upper body flat on the

desk and stick my bottom out even more. Six far harder blows landed across the full width of my bottom, and each one made my head jerk up in agony.

Then another change; she urged me to shuffle my feet wide apart and tuck my knees in. I could feel my buttocks part and closed my eyes as she tapped it firmly, right across the middle. I had a horrid feeling that the paddle would drive my cheeks further apart and some of the impact would land on my anus. It did, and a bolt of pain shot up into my insides, making me howl. Two more followed in exactly the same spot and tears filled my eyes, blurring my vision.

She gave me a brief rest, and stroked my bottom with surprising tenderness before breaking the silence.

'I don't see why I should be doing all the work,' she said. 'You can stand up and rub your own ass.'

'Thank you, ma'am,' I sobbed gratefully. My skin felt awfully hot, but the pain faded quite quickly; unlike the pain left by the cane, or even the tawse. I rubbed briskly, making my buttocks wobble.

Chrissie was filming my face and I winced convincingly. Out of the corner of my eye I saw her lower the angle of the camera and knew she was getting some shots of my thighs and sex, so I tucked my bottom in to add a bit of prominence.

Then the punishment resumed. I settled down and deliberately pushed my hips back as though inviting Betsy to do her best on me. The paddle danced quickly over the whole surface of my bottom, making it quiver and bounce and building the pain levels steadily, making it much easier to bear. She certainly knew her stuff.

I was dying to see how red she'd made me, and I guessed about the same as a nicely ripe tomato. I forget about the cameras, the video, Chrissie and Greg, and Clive and Jonquil, who were watching. I was just a very sore bum, the pain beginning to get really bad. I tried to refocus, gingerly peering over my shoulder to see what the blonde was up to. She was leaning right over my bottom and I could just see her flicking the tip of the paddle into that terribly sensitive part of me. I wanted to bring my legs together to protect myself, and especially my poor little punished bottom-hole. But I just hadn't the strength any more. All I could do was lie there and take it, whimpering continuously.

Oh, she eased my right buttock further away with her free hand, opening me right up. I bit into my bottom lip, but the extra discomfort actually relaxed me just a little, and I hoped Greg was up close, catching it all in perfect detail.

She was smacking around the rim of my anus with unerring accuracy, and then she let go. 'Six more hard ones,' she decreed, 'and then that's it.'

'Th-thank you, ma'am,' I whispered pitifully, feeling genuinely sorry for myself beneath her onslaught.

The last six were hard to take, but they were also the best of them all and I rather ruefully acknowledged that I was beginning to get off on the severity of the punishment.

Betsy left me over the table, panting heavily, my bare bottom glowing like a beacon while she entered the details in a punishment book, then the film faded out.

The scene continued with me once again in bed, fast

asleep. The lights snapped on, the ghosts hauled me up and frogmarched me out of the bedroom again, my wails of dismayed protest fading.

We reappeared in a sparse room. My wrists were tied together, the cord thrown over a beam and tightened until I was nearly on tiptoe, and then the other end was tied to a cleat on the wall. My pyjama trousers were pulled down and my bare bottom thrashed with a martinet. If I made too much noise or didn't keep reasonably still, I received three vicious strikes on the front of my thighs.

After they'd finished with me I was untied, thrown over Clive's shoulder and carried back to my room, with Jonquil happily smacking my striped bottom for good measure.

The next scene started with me in a long transparent nightie. I lay face down on the bed going through the contents of a wallet and greedily counting the thick wad of money. Then I hid it under the pillow, turned out the light, and went to sleep.

The ghosts appeared, hauled me roughly out of bed and, with icy venom, accused me of common theft, cutting short my denials by producing the evidence from beneath my pillow. They then led me away once more, we focussed in to my bottom in lightweight slacks that hugged the curves very nicely, and panned back a little to show the handcuffs I was now wearing.

'There is no excuse, young lady,' a rather pompous voice intoned. 'The owner of the wallet could easily of been contacted by you. Even had it not contained several of his business cards, you should have handed it in to the police. I therefore sentence you to a sound thrashing. This will be administered to your naked buttocks with a birch. Take the wretched girl away and prepare her. The punishment will be carried out at noon.'

When I heard the sentence my buttocks clenched and my hands shook, but I didn't make a sound as a female guard in a neat white blouse and tight black skirt led me out. The camera followed her formally clad rear and my naked one until we emerged in the open, and I then had to stand and watch while Susan, playing another miscreant, was whipped, with shots of my terrified face cut in with the other victim's reddening bottom.

Greg had added an extra element to the pillory set-up to make it more flexible. Briefly, he made a special bench, which could be divided so that the victim could either be put down flat on his or her stomach or, with the rear portion removed, made to kneel on the low platform remaining. As a final refinement, the knees could be drawn apart, moved forward and hooked over two projections, presenting the audience with a very rude display indeed.

Susan was put in all three positions, and the mounting horror in my expression as more and more of her shapely rump was revealed needed little acting ability. At last she was untied, helped to her feet and led away. Like me she was naked and I saw the red friction marks on her breasts, tummy and thighs. My head turned as she passed me and I gasped as I saw more closely the colour of her punished bottom, which the camera followed out of sight.

A firm hand then took my elbow and dragged me

forward. One camera stayed focused on my bottom, the other on my front as I walk on unsteady legs. I was helped onto the bench, my neck and wrists put in the hollows, and the top half of the actual pillory lowered and locked and then I was securely fastened down at waist and ankles.

I felt utterly helpless as the two men about to whip me mauled my bottom, assessing the quality of the flesh and the position of my exposed buttocks. I whimpered a protest and was brusquely told to be quiet.

My punishment commenced, with the cameras as usual catching the action both fore and aft. We saw one of the birches hovering over my clenched buttocks, and also the expression of real terror on my face. The first stroke landed with a vicious *thwick*, the twigs spreading on impact and bouncing off my tight cheeks, and the camera caught the huge relief on my face as the pain was less than I'd anticipated.

My bottom relaxed and my expression showed I was cautiously enjoying the experience as the birches landed in a steady rhythm, moving down to the tops of my thighs and back up again. The pattern of stripes and dots spread remorselessly and the more distant shots showed I was already quite red. My face, framed by the pillory, began to show it was starting to hurt, and my imprisoned hands added to the growing evidence of the effectiveness of the punishment. My fingers twitched and clawed impulsively at the air, and I began to gasp and breathe heavily as bits of twig flew off the ends of the birches as they hit me harder and harder.

The pain was growing. I bounced my bottom up and

down as well as tightened my buttocks and the new sound of my tummy and thighs slapping against the bench was added to the chorus of my cries and the *thwick* of birch twig on naked bottom flesh.

My tormentors then nodded at each other, tossed their worn rods to the ground, inspected my bottom and then carefully repositioned me for stage two.

When they stopped whipping me I thanked them for being merciful and promised never to steal again, but Jonquil and Clive suddenly materialised by my head, stared into my eyes and gloatingly informed me that I'd only had a third of the punishment due. I begged for mercy, their hooded heads shook in rejection of my pleas and I began to sob as my chastisers removed the lower part of the bench, leaving me kneeling with my bottom sticking out and horribly vulnerable.

Seen from behind in that position it looked a lot broader. My buttocks were marked and quite red, with a pure white strip down the centre, showing how my new position had eased then apart. My engorged sex peeped moistly from between the tops of my thighs.

The men selected longer, whippier birches and got to work again, and the combined effect of the new rods and tauter skin was immediately apparent. My bottom rolled from side to side, tucked in and then pushed out again in an obscene parody of sex, looking for all the world as if the invisible man was taking me from behind.

My bottom got redder and blotchier as the weals and livid dots left by the tips joined and merged. My cries got louder and louder, and the men hit me harder and harder.

The cameras moved smoothly round, capturing every inch of exposed flesh, every twitch and every stripe, but just when genuine tears were beginning to meander down my cheeks the rods were cast aside. I felt hands grip my legs and pull them apart and then up towards my face. I felt my buttocks move apart and tighten up and whimpered pleas at my tormentors as I struggled vainly, but my buttocks were resoundingly slapped and I sobbed my apologies. A strap was then fixed tightly around my waist, so I could hardly move a muscle. There was a brief pause while my poor bottom was inspected and then new birches were picked up and the third phase got underway, the men concentrating on the nearest buttock so that the tips bit agonisingly into my open cleft and my howls filled the warm summer air.

I was completely helpless. My hands dangled limply from the holes in the pillory, my head jerked with each short stroke, the tears flowed down my cheeks. Inevitably my poor anus and sex lips caught the occasional sharp nip and there was nothing I could do to protect either.

At last it was thought I'd been suitably punished and I was set free. The cameras closed in to capture my glistening tears and the changing shape of my bottom as it was restored to something approaching decency.

Chrissie walked backwards in front of me as I was led away from the pillory, and Greg followed. I was led indoors to another room, and guided face down onto a couch. Jane examined my bottom with professional interest and applied some cream, while the camera cut from her soothing hands to my tear streaked face.

'I'll never, ever, steal again,' I whispered, and the camera cut to Clive and Jonquil, nodding their approval.

As I said, all this took several weeks to plan and film, with the several enforced breaks to give my bottom time to get back to normal.

Luckily, both Chrissie and I were kept busy. The campaign for the new car had gone down well and we were asked to redesign a new brochure, work up an intensive press campaign and to come with some ideas for more TV ads. The brochure was a nice little challenge as we had a bit of a battle to get the client to do something different to the normal glossy number, but as the car was more practical than beautiful, we had a good case anyway. My new computer was brought in to produce the finished roughs and they were good enough to win the argument.

For the commercials we hit on the idea of short snappy ads, mainly of talking heads, so that the production costs were minimal. Apart from earning the agency quite a few brownie points for economical use of their budget, we were also convinced they would work. Each film highlighted a feature of the car, but without labouring the point.

Most used the device of someone on the phone. For example, a young woman talking to a friend and reassuring her that she would easily be able to get three kids and all their stuff in for a day on the beach. Or the same actress claiming she'd done an undefined trip in less than an hour and vehemently denying that she broke the speed limit.

All the films finished on a simple product shot with a voice-over repeating the main selling point of the film, cutting to the company logo.

Chrissie and I were both happy with the concept and, much to the annoyance of the media department who had to work extra hard to produce a sensible schedule, the client agreed with us.

I was earning my retainer, but even with *Nightmare Punishments* carrying our hopes for mega sales, I wanted and needed to build up a list of good CP videos as soon as possible.

Clive and I discussed future productions at some length and I welcomed his suggestions that we should include a number of shorter films, which would cost less to produce, could be sold for less than the sixty minute features I'd done up to then, and would still be better than the average competitive effort.

In one of the healing intervals I directed one of these. A youngish couple had just enjoyed what was obviously a good dinner at his flat when she insisted on doing the washing up.

'No way,' he said flatly. 'You never let me do it when I come to you, so you're not doing it here.'

'And what will you do to stop me?' she goaded, with a distinct smirk.

'I'll put you across my knee.'

'Oh, and what then?'

He frowned. 'I'm not sure. I've never had to go that far before. But I'm sure I'll think of something.' He put his arms around her and let his hands drop to the seat of her tight skirt and squeeze speculatively. 'I've got it,' he went on eagerly. 'I'll spank you.'

'Will you really?' she purred. 'You sadistic, chauvinist pig.'

'And for that insult, I'll lift your skirt.'

'No you won't.'

'And after a few smacks on your knickers, I'll pull them down and do it on your bare bottom.'

'Oh, no you won't,' she repeated.

'Then I'll strip you naked, make you kneel on the sofa with your bum sticking right out and give you even more.'

She shook her head determinedly. 'No you won't.'

'And when I've had enough, I'll take you to the bedroom and screw you.'

She shook her head again, but this time with less conviction, so he took his opportunity and led her to a chair, put her across his knee and did exactly as promised. She had a lovely round bottom and he looked at it, felt and smacked it with evident relish, while she cooed and purred at the strokes and protested with a distinct lack of conviction.

After a few minutes it was quite clear that she was getting turned on and he began to spank her properly until her bottom was a beautiful rich red all over. He sat back, contemplated it and pronounced himself very satisfied.

She peered up at him over her shoulder. 'Are you finished with me?' she asked meekly with wide-eyed innocence, but then it moved on to the next part of the threatened treatment. She was stripped naked, led to the sofa and made to kneel up on the seat, head down, bottom up, with her gorgeous shaved sex on view.

A volley of hefty spanks made her wriggle and squirm, but then he claimed his hand was sore.

'So's my bottom!' she wailed, but significantly kept it in position.

'That's the whole point,' he replied as he disappeared into the kitchen, emerging after a few seconds with an evil grin and a big wooden spoon.

A couple of dozen with that and she'd really had enough. She stood up, peered over her shoulder, ruefully rubbing the mass of scarlet splotches covering her bottom and then smiled impishly up at him, licking her lips suggestively to remind him of what came next.

'Now you can do the washing up,' he said dismissively.

'You…' but she held her tongue, and a couple of minutes of varied close-ups of her spectacularly marked bottom as she obeyed and then turned to him, wiping her hands on a tea-towel.

'If you still want to screw me,' she said mischievously, 'you'll have to catch me first,' and then she dodged away from him and scurried out of the kitchen, with Greg's camera following. Her lovely bottom wobbled more than I would have expected as she fled, giggling, and it was such a lovely sight that I closed the film on a slow motion repeat, with her squeals of delight changing to moans of pleasure in the background.

That is still one of my favourite videos. It really does show how spanking can be fun and sexy and the couple were brilliant. They were very much into the scene and carried on as if the cameras weren't there, which made it all natural and convincing.

One surprising but welcome visitor to my cottage was Roger, the man I'd met at Clive and Jonquil's when I previewed *College Tails*. I hadn't been able to talk to him properly then, but had seen enough to be intrigued by him, and so I was delighted when he dropped in. I was even happier when I discovered he only lived about ten miles away from me. But I was rather deflated, however, when he mentioned his wife.

Although Chrissie and I were completely happy together, I was beginning to feel the need for an occasional man. Greg was great but he only wanted to shag my bottom, which was fine, but I was missing having a man in the more conventional way.

Not surprisingly, we soon got talking about CP and his comments on my videos were encouraging and helpful. I had just finished editing *His Lover's Tail*, as described above, and was due to take the master tape to Clive and Jonquil the following day, and as Roger mentioned how much pleasure he got from watching his wife walking bare-bottomed, I thought I would give him a sneak preview in the hope that he'd particularly like the chase sequence.

And he certainly did, and asked me to play it again. Then he told me that his wife was a keen and good tennis player, and as Wimbledon was on television, he asked if we could watch a little, so we did. There was a key ladies match on at the time, and even though tennis was not high in my list of interests, I had to admit that with my newfound enthusiasm for the female bottom, I actually quite enjoyed it.

At one point I cursed the director for pulling away

from a promising shot of a nicely oscillating rear and cutting to a crowd shot. Roger grinned at me, and then asked the favour he'd been leading up to all along.

Basically, it was to film his wife and one of her friends playing tennis on their own secluded court, bare bottoms to the fore, of course.

Naturally I agreed, asked if Chrissie could come along with a second camera, he agreed and we fixed a date and time, weather permitting.

Roger's wife was a bit overpowering at first; tall, blonde, bouncy, and more than a little posh.

'Hello,' she cried theatrically when we arrived on the appointed day. 'Super to see you both.' But she was actually a very nice, warm friendly woman and we were soon getting on like a house on fire. Her friend was just as nice, although a lot quieter, slimmer and darker. In their warm company I relaxed and started to enjoy the day. The girls suggested that I should start off by filming them getting changed with Susie, the friend, forgetting her knickers and Jilly, Roger's wife, suggesting they both play without any. They then entered into the spirit with such enthusiasm that I soon realised there was far more to both than met the eye, and began to really like them.

The finished video pleased all concerned, even me, and certainly showed Jilly to good advantage. I had spent more time filming her than Susie, catching most of the action from behind her and getting some excellent shots of her firm round bottom peeping from under the hem of her very short white skirt. Especially when she was stretching to serve or pick up a stray ball.

To progress the action, Susie's skirt slid down to her feet after a couple of games – the zip had broken – and Jilly nobly suggested that she should take hers off too so she wouldn't have the advantage of decency, and as it was a beautifully hot and sunny day, both girls ended up in just their white tennis shoes, adding further interest to the proceedings.

Then to add a bit of variety I made Chrissie strip off to act as a highly unorthodox ball girl, and she then thought it would be splendid if she took a few shots of me doing the same. Not being anything like as athletic I wasn't very good at it, and Jilly seized the chance to make me bend over for a sound spanking. Jilly and Susie also agreed that the winner would spank the loser of each set, with a proper hiding for the overall loser. As we were not particularly worried about the tennis, it was quite easy to fix it so that it was apparently one set all and that Jilly won the decider.

It was fun to shoot the whole game, challenging to edit and the happy couple were delighted with the result – and I had more delicious material for my growing private collection.

And, even better, when I showed them the finished result, Roger offered me a generous fee, which I refused as I preferred to think of them as friends, not business contacts.

'But I must give you something,' Roger insisted, and the couple of bottles of an excellent red wine we'd enjoyed by then explains why I dreamily said something about longing for a proper screw.

'Roger would be delighted to oblige!' Jilly exclaimed

eagerly, and I looked at her dumbly, unable to believe that she was actually volunteering her husband's services.

She grinned at me. 'I've often wondered what he'd look like on the job. Now's my chance to find out.'

Well, if she was happy, I was too, and Roger was looking at me with unmistakable anticipation. So, it was clothes off and up to their lovely bedroom, dominated by a super king-size brass bed.

It was great. The best I had ever had with a man. Actually the best bit was the second one, when Jilly and I got together to give Roger something to remember. He lay on his back, I straddled his middle, and Jilly guided him inside me and then sat on his face. I pumped my hips up and down on his very impressive shaft, she ground hers over his busy mouth, and she and I kissed and played with each other's breasts and clits. It was heaven!

And what made the adventure even better was that both of them were sorry Chrissie had not been able to join us, and made me promise to bring her next time. The thought that they wanted a next time was great and made a lot better by the prospect of sharing it all with my girlfriend.

Editing *Nightmare Punishments* was much easier than I had anticipated. Partly because I was much more confident by then, but it also helped that I had not actually been behind the camera and so I was seeing it for the first time.

As Chrissie had been so heavily involved, I asked her

to come with me and we stayed with Clive and Jonquil for a whole weekend, using the agency's facilities during the day and having the pleasure of their company in the evenings.

I was very pleased with the video. It took me a bit of time to view all the scenes from an editor's point of view, as I was rather intrigued by my own performance in general and my bare bottom in particular. But as I had a clear idea of how the finished film should look, once I reached the proper level of objectivity I was selecting and adapting, cutting and shutting with an increasingly sure touch.

Well ahead of schedule, the two of us ran through the final version and, as I watched it, I felt a surge of strength and new purpose. It was probably because I'd spent several weeks in self-imposed submission and I'd suddenly shaken off the chains and wanted to experience the other side of the coin more fully than before.

Our surroundings also acted as a trigger. Both Chrissie and I had been spanked several times in that room and for me of course, it was the scene of my initiation. As I rewound the tape I knew I had to give in to temptation.

'Right, Chrissie,' I said quietly. 'I'd like to discuss your camera work.' I think the darling girl sensed immediately what was going through my mind, as her face fell and she sat very still. I mentioned that she had twice overshot while panning in, and although it had been perfectly easy to edit the last few frames out, it was careless of her.

'Otherwise, you did very well,' I reassured her, 'but if you want to help out again you are really going to have to learn how to do it without a hitch. And we both know the best way of learning, don't we, Chrissie?'

'Yes, Lucy,' she said meekly.

'Good, in that case I'm going to take your jeans down, put you across my knee, pull your knickers down and give you a really hard spanking on your bare bottom.'

Obviously there was absolutely no need to have said anything. I could simply have pointed down at my lap and she would have bent over it without a murmur. But I thoroughly enjoyed going into gory detail and was in no mood to deny myself one of life's little pleasures. And I freely admit that I made a real meal of spanking her, undressing her slowly, feeling her exposed flesh to my heart's content.

Her position on my lap needed some adjustment, as her adorable little pink bottom-hole just had to be examined, stroked and penetrated. Her lovely soft, smooth, white, beautifully posed buttocks had to be spanked and spanked until they were a uniform blotchy red from base to apex.

Then, after she had been cuddled and kissed better, she had to kiss the hand that had spanked her, the thighs she had laid across and the bottom that had been squashed by our combined weight. Then I sat on her face, shifting back and forward to have her busy tongue on both holes, while my hands were happily occupied between her legs.

My thirst for Chrissie was eased but not quenched by dominating her. On our way back to the Docklands flat, we idly discussed the possibilities of leaving the tape with Clive and Jonquil and going home, but decided it would be stupid not to see their reaction to it, even bad manners, and not in our best interests to miss one of Jonquil's dinners. So we stayed, and they loved the video.

And, even though I had only seen it a couple of hours beforehand, I found no reason to alter my initial satisfaction with it. The fact that the nice make-up girl had made me look so different it was like watching a stranger helped, but the main thing was that Greg had lit and framed everything so well that the feeling of being in a horribly realistic nightmare was very vivid. Clive and Jonquil were excellent and their looming presence and calm authority was genuinely scary.

I was also pleased with the pace of the action. The five sequences were different enough to make each involving in its own right, and at the same time the build up to the climax was inexorable.

The punishment scenes came out as hoped. There was variety of situation, implement, position and preparation. My acting was not too embarrassing and I showed the progression from outrage to rueful acceptance quite well.

The other girls added a lot to the interest and, if none of them showed me up too badly, neither did they let anyone down.

During dinner we discussed plans for the next production and eventually agreed on another *College Tails*. To make a change we would have a visiting salesman calling on Susan to try and get her to add to her range of spanking implements. These would have to be tried out, of course, both as wielder and recipient, so Susan's opulent bottom would feature strongly and, to allow her to get the hang of them, the games mistress would be a willing volunteer. Her final choice would then be put to use on a couple of naughty pupils. It sounded great and I really looked forward to making it.

To finish the evening on a suitably upbeat note, Clive asked me if I would like a special reward for my work on *Nightmare*, and to everyone's surprise I didn't ask for the sensual punishment I think everyone expected, but to put Jonquil across my knee.

Clive looked delighted, Chrissie amused and respectful and Jonquil resigned. I think, in retrospect, that she had already assumed I had moved out of her reach and influence, but partly out of gratitude for my work and partly because there was a bit of the submissive in her, she agreed quite willingly.

It was very satisfying indeed; her bottom was gorgeous. It quivered enticingly under my reasonable assault and coloured beautifully. She didn't wriggle and cry out like my girlfriend, but that didn't worry me. I wanted to show that I was now on a much more even footing as far as she was concerned, not to hurt her unduly. And to ease her worries, as soon as she had stopped rubbing her bottom I undressed her completely, sat her down and lay across her lap. She got the message and I received a lovely warm spanking as well.

Next morning Chrissie and I left with hangovers, generous royalty cheques, and the promise of a well-deserved week's holiday.

Chapter Six

If I had known what the end of that summer would bring I am quite sure I wouldn't have enjoyed our break nearly as much. Not that we indulged in a prolonged orgy of sex and spanking – no, rather the opposite.

We pottered, walking in the local woods; we met friends at the local pub and had several round for drinks and barbecues; we explored Rye after long walks along Camber Sands, and basically, we chilled out and thoroughly enjoyed getting away from the various pressures for a while.

As the weeks passed I had a lot of fun expanding my knowledge of CP, by then fully accepting that I was addicted to the complex pleasures of the whole gorgeous concept. I began to need stronger doses of pain and humiliation even more than I needed the high of domination. Chrissie and I, as always, were in near perfect harmony, and with her help and encouragement I was increasingly content.

When we were both in the mood, even the slightest mistake or aggravation meant an involved and painful punishment, always containing those basic and essential elements that turned us on so easily.

But we didn't need to be naughty to be punished. We both enjoyed it – giving and receiving.

One morning I came back from the village to find Chrissie getting in a bit of practice with the cane on a particularly padded cushion reserved for that worthy purpose, and which was looking increasingly battered by then. She was wearing only a T-shirt and thong, and looking even more delicious than usual. I watched her from the doorway for a couple of minutes; the graceful movements of arm and body; the visible sway of her breasts, obviously naked under her tight shirt; the way the lower curves of her buttocks peeped out when she raised her arm; the intense concentration on her face, all combined to make me breathlessly excited.

'Hi, Juicy,' she smiled, when she saw me. 'Fancy a go?'

She told me later that she was actually offering me the cane and cushion but instead, with all the usual symptoms of trepidation and arousal, I took down my jeans and knickers, shuffled over to the chair, tossed the dented cushion on the floor and bent right over, tucking my knees in and dipping my back to offer her a nicely rounded and spread bottom.

She accepted the offer in eloquent silence and beat me hard and methodically until every accessible inch of my rump was red and striped, and then we went to bed so she could soothe me better with a tub of cold cream.

Later that day I wanted to do the same to her, and true to form she did not protest, just asked me how I wanted her positioned. I bared her bottom as lovingly as ever, and guided her into position over the kitchen table, her upper half flat to it, her legs parted slightly and straight, her bottom beautifully curved and ready at

172

my mercy.

I tapped her with the cane, not just getting my distance but also taking full advantage of the opportunity to revel in everything from the view of her to the feel of the cane gently vibrating in my hand. She turned her face to me and, although her arm hid the lower half, I could see her eyes, softly pleading with me to hurry up and get on with it – to beat her hard.

So I gave her a full dozen. Nowhere near full strength, but each one had her rising up on her elbows and toes, her face contorted with pain and the breath hissing from her lungs, and I saw her knuckles turn white as she clung to the furthest edge of the table. As I neared the twelfth stroke she tried bravely to blink away her tears. I smiled encouragement at her and she pouted ruefully back before courageously offering her suffering bottom again.

I crouched down beside her, gazing happily at the rising red weals and the faint pink flush on her skin between the stripes, running my fingertips over the raised tramline marks, and to make it even worse for her I firmly forced her cheeks apart, gripping tightly to renew the burning sting and have a long look at her twitching little bottom-hole.

I was much more accurate by then, with the confidence to make her move her feet together so her legs were at right angles to her torso and she was up on tiptoe. Then I carefully aimed at the junction of thighs and buttocks, at those lovely sensitive folds of hers.

I swept the cane down and knew it was exquisitely painful for her. She closed her eyes, whimpering softly, her thighs trembling with stress and fear and delight, and once the allotted twelve had been administered she straightened up quickly and rubbed her poor punished buttocks, nibbling her lower lip cutely as she felt how pronounced the weals were and starting the soothing process, which I then continued.

One day we went up to Jane's consulting rooms again and stripped naked while she indulged her hitherto secret fantasies with our offered bodies, and I enjoyed this second visit much more than the first.

She gave us a sophisticated enema kit, with a choice of nozzles, one shaped like a slender cock, so we treated each other once a week, enjoyed both the giving and the receiving and felt the benefits. And the kit also inspired another imaginative video.

The opening shot was of a pretty dark-haired girl in a tight mini-skirt, walking slowly down a typical London side street, obviously looking for a specific address. She moved past the camera, which turned with her, and she moved far enough for her full length to be in shot, and then we panned in to a close-up of the seat of her skirt. She was promisingly curved and her rump swayed enticingly as she walked.

She found the address, walked up the few steps to the front door, rang the bell, said a few words into a speaker by the door, waited for a second, pushed the door open and went inside.

We filmed her sitting nervously in a small, sparsely furnished room. An older woman in a white coat came in, sat down next to the girl, picked up a clipboard and began talking to her, their heads intimately close. We heard their voices but not what they were saying, until we panned in, at which point the older woman was reassuring the girl.

'It can be a little embarrassing but not at all painful – and really very beneficial,' she said, and the girl nodded cautiously.

'Good,' the woman went on. 'Now if you could just slip your panties down and bend over a little, I'll check your bottom.'

Bright red in the face, the girl stood, turned, inched up her short skirt and eased her knickers down to the tops of her thighs before bending from the waist and putting her hands on her knees. We then panned in to close-up side view of her bare bottom and flushed face, then cut to a view behind the woman as she reached out, touched the very pretty buttocks, and her thumbs pressed in on either side of the tight deep cleft and slowly opened it up, exposing a neat dark anus.

'That's fine, dear,' the woman said. 'Now if you would please take all your clothes off.'

'Everything?' the girl asked with obvious dismay.

'That's what I said,' came the curt reply, a hint of steel in the tone.

The pretty girl obeyed sulkily and then they walked into another room, with the camera naturally following the girl's bottom. They were now in a simple room with a low table, a couch, a basin and a couple of straight-backed chairs. The enema kit was on the table and the woman calmly and sympathetically explained the process, to which the girl pulled the occasional face, but was apparently resigned to her treatment.

The woman asked her which position she would like to take up and, when the girl looked blank, suggested either lying on her side with her knees drawn up, or kneeling.

The girl shrugged. 'I don't really know,' she said meekly, so the woman suggested she should try both and see which she found more comfortable.

Eventually the woman suggested that kneeling up was preferable as she could then see what she was doing more easily, and the girl obeyed without protest, sticking her bottom out nicely. She was then carefully lubricated, with shots from back and side, the former showing her taut buttocks and the busy finger, the latter showing the expression of intent on the woman's face and the girl's growing realisation that it was definitely a case of so far, so good.

We then cut from the woman's hands filling the enema to the waiting bottom and back, with a closer viewpoint each time, until the last two shots consisted of the glistening nozzle, with a drop of cloudy water oozing suggestively from the tip and then the girl's anus, which gave a lovely nervous little twitch.

The insertion was shown from two angles, from the side, so that the viewer could see the tube sliding in between the girl's rounded buttocks, her face screwed up in anticipation, clearing as it proved to be pleasant rather than painful, from over the woman's shoulder.

As the enema was administered we moved from the rear view with the woman's hand actually pumping the water in the foreground and the girl's bottom filling the background, to the same side view, every now and then panning to a close-up of her face, showing her gradual agitation as the water filled her bowels.

She complained of cramps, so the woman stopped pumping and massaged her tummy with one hand and her buttocks with the other, and the girl's expression changed from dismay to relief. 'Ooooh, that's better,' she sighed sweetly, and noticeably urged her bottom out for the woman.

When the two pints had been pumped in, we saw the tube being slowly extracted and the girl's face making it quite clear that she liked feeling it slipping out of her rectum. She was then made to stay in position for a couple of minutes, and she began to shuffle about on her knees and moan softly as the need to get rid of the water grew.

Then the woman gave her a ringing slap on the bottom and told her she could get down, so she clambered gingerly down from the examination couch and looked frantically around for the toilet. The woman apologised for not having told her before where it was, and led the way out of the room, down a short corridor and into a bathroom, the camera following the girl closely as she walked with stiff-legged urgency, and we thought that was the appropriate time to cut.

Then back to the treatment room, and the woman asked the girl how she felt.

'Fantastic,' the girl enthused.

'I told you the benefits were worth it,' said the woman, and then gave the girl permission to get dressed as we faded out.

It was a fun little video to make – especially as Greg got particularly excited during the filming for some reason, and when the others had left he whispered in my ear that he just *had* to have his wicked way with me. So as I leaned over the couch, with Greg's lovely thick cock reaming my back passage with all his customary skill and enthusiasm, I felt that all was pretty much well with the world.

A few days later I had a call from Clive who told me that Morganna wanted to see me again. As soon as he mentioned her name, my complacency disappeared. Although my first time with her had not been quite as bad as I'd feared, and she had taught me that I could take far more discomfort and humiliation than I'd imagined, I had vowed that I would never go back to her on the same basis.

So I said as much to Clive, and he expressed surprise and a degree of displeasure at my reticence. He didn't threaten me with anything specific, but I knew him well enough to appreciate that it was better to stay in his good books.

I agreed very reluctantly, rang her to make a date and, on the appointed hour, went a little apprehensively to her discreet rooms in a Soho side street. I had thought long and hard during the journey, trying to identify why I was basically afraid of Morganna. It was partly her character and appearance, of course; her jet-black hair, pure white skin, glinting eyes and cruel mouth made her pretty awe-inspiring at the best of times, and her normal choice of clothes – skin-tight, black, and usually leather

– did nothing to make her any less alarming. On the other hand, she had been pretty considerate during my visit to her. She could have, for example, just lashed into my bottom with the sjambok and not warned me that it was at the extreme end in the range of disciplinary weapons, let alone actually ask me whether I was up for it.

I eventually worked out that my main reason for wanting to avoid her was that I didn't feel she liked me. She certainly desired me, but I always felt that, as far as she was concerned, I was a body not a person, whereas Chrissie, Jonquil, Susan, Jane, Clive and Greg genuinely liked, and in some cases, really cared for me. All of them enjoyed humiliating and hurting me, but they knew I enjoyed being humiliated and hurt – by them. Even Roger and Jilly seemed to enjoy my company, and were as warm and interested in me when the atmosphere was innocent as when it was not so.

Morganna wasn't really turned on by spanking and I was. It was then – and still is – just about my favourite sexual activity other than actually screwing, and even then there were and are times when I would rather be lovingly and sensually spanked than bonked. Chrissie, Jonquil and Susan knew how to spank me. Lots of dialogue on the subject of my naughtiness, detailed descriptions of my imminent ordeal, lots of comments and fondling of my buttocks before, during and after they had been bared, and then a slow, steady spanking, giving me plenty of time to appreciate my nudity, the feel of soft thighs beneath me, the sound of a stiff palm hitting my vulnerable flesh, the quivers and wobbles and, gradually, the scorching pain.

It was always delicious with them… but Morganna just scared me.

So I walked through the narrow Soho streets with my heart in my dry mouth, my palms damp, my bottom feeling heavy and awkward, its usual carefree sway changed to a cumbersome waddle. Or so it felt to me. I heard a low whistle behind me and, as I appeared to be the only girl around, assumed it was in honour of my rear and felt a little better.

But as I approached the alleyway leading to Morganna's place, I became increasingly aware that my sex was damp, and it struck me that the fear of the imminent ordeal was actually exciting me.

As I rang the doorbell there was a bitter taste in my mouth as I finally came to terms with an aspect of my character I'd been trying to keep completely buried.

I was stripped, turned this way and that, forced into any number of increasingly revealing positions and nearly always kept there with the help of her range of ropes, chains, bars and pulleys. And there were two things that were particularly memorable and exciting. The first was that she put a tight leather helmet on me, which covered my head and face, except for a hole for my nose and a removable strip over my mouth. Every so often she would open the strip and either kiss me passionately, or get me to kiss and lick whichever part of her she felt needed attention. Her breasts, buttocks, thighs, sex and anus all demanded my homage. I didn't really mind, I suppose, as she had lovely smooth skin, was perfectly clean, and tasted very nice. I couldn't see a thing, which made me feel especially helpless, but as time went on I began to find the smell of leather a real turn on. I had always rather enjoyed smelling Chrissie immediately after I'd taken her leather trousers down, but this was much more intense.

Secondly, she did one thing to me that almost makes me come every time I think about it.

She had me lying on my back on some sort of a bench or table, fixed a leg spreader to my ankles and then brought my knees back and roped them separately to, I assumed, the legs of whatever I was lying on. She had already beaten my naked bottom quite severely, using what felt like a couple of paddles, one probably leather and the other certainly wood, and had whipped me with something thin, biting and excruciatingly painful. I groaned as she doubled me up and the flesh of my buttocks stretched, sending new waves of agony through me.

She then pushed a cushion under the small of my back. I tensed, knowing full well that her eyes would be glued to my fully exposed anus and sex and absolutely sure that she had every intention of hitting me there. I trusted her not to do me any damage, but was still almost wetting myself with consternation.

Time seemed to stand still. My breathing was difficult enough anyway, without the added problem of feeling really uneasy. Then I jumped when something brushed against my anus. I was panting hard, my nostrils flared as the strip over my mouth was firmly in place. I felt something else touch me in the same place, and gasped because it didn't hurt. In fact, it was fantastic! Not as good as Chrissie's tongue, but not far short. Whatever it was, it was dry and tickly. A feather? I hoped it was and gradually all the tension left me as I lay back and enjoyed the experience. She circled it around my private opening, and then slowly inwards until I really did feel as though it was just inside my back passage. My burning buttocks faded into the background and I heard myself groaning with sheer lust as the tantalising little object probed further...

And then I screamed pitifully into the leather gag when she stopped and the pleasure was replaced with a sharp pain right where she'd been tickling me. And then again, six times in all.

Then the feather returned, feeling even more blissful on my punished anus.

I lost count of the times she moved from one implement to the other; my bottom was a sea of conflicting sensations and I was totally spaced out by the intensity of it all.

Then I felt another surge of panic as I felt her fingers touching the engorged lips of my sex, easing them apart. The gloved fingers of one hand held me open and the fingers of the other teased my clitoris until I was writhing hopelessly as waves of pleasure engulfed me, like the pounding surf I remembered one stormy day in the past, walking along a beach in north Cornwall.

I think she even slapped my exposed sex. Not hard, but hard enough to make me shudder, and I could feel my wet labia pulse as warm pain enhanced the thrills.

Then her attention moved back to my bottom and the feather, and then to my clitty until I was really straining against the ropes, bars and chains, my muffled shrieks increasing in intensity. Then I shrieked into the gag as she cruelly pressed a huge vibrator into my bottom and switched it on, turning me on even more, and I came so strongly that I actually passed out for a few moments.

Once slightly recovered I was suspended by my wrists, and she used several implements to beat my bottom. But I was beyond caring. I just hung there, the smell of leather as intoxicating as ever, the cheeks of my bottom trembling violently as they were hit with remorseless skill.

After a weary journey home I fell into bed. Chrissie came up with a jar of our magic ointment and cooed happily over all my marks as she kissed and soothed them. I told her about the feather, and promised faithfully to show her what it was like.

Chapter Seven

Ever since the tennis video we'd seen a lot more of Roger and Jilly. Both Chrissie and I enjoyed men too, and although I still liked and respected Greg enormously, his fixation with my bottom made his sexual appeal rather limited. What made doing it with Roger extra special was that Jilly not only raised no objections to his extra-marital activities, but also loved being involved.

One morning when Chrissie was at a meeting at the agency, she rang up, saying Roger was away, it was a lovely day, she was bored out of her skull and would I like to come round for a swim.

'I'm on my way,' I replied happily, 'as soon as I've found my bikini.'

'Please don't bother,' Jilly said quickly. 'I love swimming naked, if you don't mind. And our pool's totally secluded.'

'Fine,' I said, 'that sounds like fun.'

They also had remote control gates and as I climbed out of the car to announce my presence, I realised that my knickers were very damp indeed. This rather surprised me, for although Jilly was very sexy, I associated her completely with Roger and hadn't even dreamt of any intimate hanky-panky with her. I was looking forward to seeing her naked again, but more for the aesthetic satisfaction than anything else.

'Hi, it's Lucy,' I replied to the buzz.

'Hi, you *have* been quick,' came her metallic response. 'Come on in.'

As I drove up to their lovely old house I had a wicked thought, so I pulled to a halt, nipped out, tore off the light summer dress and knickers which was all that I was wearing, got back in, parked the car and, with my heart in my mouth in case she had an unexpected visitor, rang the doorbell.

The front door opened a little, and I could see part of her lovely blonde hair and a twinkling blue eye. It widened in surprise, the door also opened wide, and there was Jilly, as naked as I was.

We grinned at each other, had a very promising kiss, separated breathlessly and then she took my hand and we went out to the pool. It was a thoroughly enjoyable day and it wasn't until a lot later that I cottoned on to the fact that I had been almost on trial, but as I drove home, feeling deliciously weary and tanned after the best part of a day spent in and around the pool, I just had another of those relatively rare but very precious moods of pure contentment.

Jilly was as much fun as I expected her to be, but much more forthcoming, and I really did feel that I had made a good friend. She admitted to me that she only liked girls as an occasional diversion, as Roger satisfied almost all her needs, both physical and mental.

If I had been hoping for a bit of a saucy session, I may well have been disappointed with that snippet of news, but as it was I took another sip of my iced drink and felt pleased for her. She asked me quite a few questions about our lives and pastimes, which I answered more or less fully and truthfully, letting slip that there was a bit more between Chrissie and me than I really wanted a relative stranger to know. I was a little angry with myself for saying too much, and promised to confess to Chrissie that evening and take the inevitable spanking with good grace.

It was only some time afterwards that I realised Jilly had asked me several apparently innocent questions and that my answers had inexorably led her to get me into a rare form of sexual excitement which I was eventually to fall for hook, line and sinker.

Perhaps if I hadn't had to confess my indiscretions to Chrissie and if I hadn't found that she'd forgotten to pay the phone bill so we were in danger of being disconnected, I might have thought a bit more deeply about the events of that day. Why had Jilly asked me so probingly whether I liked riding? Even when I said that my only experiences on horseback had been as a girl, spending holidays with relations in Ireland. Since then, I told her, I had come to an arrangement with horses – if I didn't get on their backs, they wouldn't throw me off.

She had also wanted to know far more than even I was willing to tell her about my more outlandish sexual experiences and tastes, but I must have either hinted at more than I realised or, and more probably, Roger had heard quite a bit from Clive and Jonquil and told her at least some of the details. She ended up by asking if she could give me a little spanking, and I clambered across her naked lap on the firm understanding that we would then change places.

She proved to be a good spanker and an even better spankee, if that's the right word. Her sweet little bottom wobbled and reddened very prettily, and I enjoyed both sides of my favourite form of exercise so much that I ravished her afterwards. Not that she objected one little bit!

Anyway, all that was forgotten when Chrissie got home that evening. I opened a bottle of wine, made supper, we discussed her meeting and the project that was the result of it, and then I confessed my sins. Naturally she sentenced me to a sound spanking, ending up with a dozen with the wooden hairbrush. I decided I wouldn't mention the phone bill until after I'd been punished, on the basis that she would enjoy dealing with my bare bottom far more if she didn't have similar treatment awaiting hers. And, of course, when I put her across my knee, I would be sitting on very sore buttocks.

My very entertaining day must have got me really in the mood, and I was extremely pleased when Chrissie decided to make the punishment a formal one. Instead of being pulled across her knee right away, I was made to go upstairs and change into a T-shirt with just a G-string underneath.

Then I had to stand in a corner with my hands on my head, which raised the hem of the shirt just enough to expose the lower sweep of my bottom. I stared at the wall in front of me, breathing deeply and steadily, scared enough of the forthcoming pain to make me feel really alive, but not in that state of real fear which a serious beating induces.

After some time in the sun and even more in the pool,

my bottom felt soft, smooth and receptive. The back cord of the thong fitted snugly into the crack of my bottom, and when I squeezed my buttocks I could feel it against my anus, which was nice.

I heard faint rustles as Chrissie took her clothes off, and eventually it was time. I took my usual deep breath, walked over to her right side and listened while she ticked me off and reminded me what lay in store. The hem of my shirt tickled my poor buttocks and I realised I was trembling.

Then I had to lower myself over her lap, the G-string was eased down, and my shirt folded up above my waist. Then there was a long pause while she looked at my presented bottom.

My bare bottom meekly spread before her, accessible and vulnerable, ready to be punished.

And punished it was… long and hard.

I did all the usual things throughout; concentrated on the small area of carpet below my face, kept my breathing as steady as I could, and relaxed and enjoyed the tolerable pain of the overture, knowing it would get a lot worse before it got better.

'Six stingers,' she announced, her voice tight. I kept my legs in, my elbows bent, and my bottom up. I took a deep breath, expelled it immediately I felt the first blow, and couldn't help crying out.

I was whimpering after the sixth, and in tears with a ferociously sore bottom, standing back in the corner for a five-minute break before the hairbrush was introduced to the proceedings. My bottom cooled somewhat, and I was dying to rub it.

Then I was summoned again, took a slow walk to the open end of the chaise longue, and put my knees on the seat, one at a time, well apart. I bent forward and pressed my breasts into the seat, and cushioned my face on my folded arms, my bottom thrust right out, my buttocks drum-tight.

Then Chrissie took her time reducing me to a quivering, sobbing jelly. Lots and lots of sharp wristy smacks slowly raised the temperature of my bottom to boiling point.

Then I was subjected to the last straw. A finger coated with lubricant smoothed over my straining bottom-hole and then wormed its way into the tight passage beyond. It then slid out, and a sharp stab replaced the rather nice sensation as the handle of the hairbrush was pressed home. I knelt there, relieved it was all over, feeling my tears dry as the glow took over from the burning sting and, as soon as I was over the worst, could begin to look forward to the role reversal.

About a week after I spent the day with Jilly, she rang and asked if Chrissie and I would like to spend the day with them. Of course we would and we set off in high spirits, hoping for some nice action but quite happy to be conventionally sociable if that was what they wanted.

After a relaxed tour of the garden, Jilly suggested a swim. Naturally, I had forgotten to remind Chrissie to bring her costume and, needless to say, my sluttish little lover didn't bat an eyelid, stripped off, dived in and started swimming with a skill and grace which made me proud. Jilly and I watched for a while, and then joined her.

Later we had a delicious buffet lunch and lay digesting it in perfect peace and quiet in the shady areas around the pool. Then Roger broke the beautiful tranquillity of the warm afternoon.

'Have either of you heard of pony driving?' he asked.

Chrissie sat up on her lounger. 'Yes, vaguely,' she replied. 'You do mean with girls, don't you?'

'With us, invariably,' Jilly chimed in, looking at Chrissie with respect, 'although we know some who prefer boys – or a combination.'

'Tell me more,' Chrissie enthused.

I wondered what they were talking about, and not for the first time realised that compared to Chrissie, I was still innocence itself.

We went for a walk, Roger in his trunks, we girls naked, across a courtyard to some rather derelict outbuildings. Roger fiddled with a small keypad hidden behind a clematis and opened a heavy door.

We went inside and I was now bewildered. Facing us was a row of four tiny carts, each one with its slender shafts pointing upwards like a praying mantis. I then noticed the racks on another wall and gawped. The array of long thin whips made me clench my buttocks instinctively, but it was the strange sight of several indefinable pieces of what looked like black leather, all with coloured plumes dangling limply down which threw me. Equally puzzling was another row of what looked suspiciously like horses' tails, again in various colours.

'Wow!' Chrissie exclaimed, her eyes shining in the gloom.

'What the…?' I gasped.

190

Beaming happily Roger and Jilly began to explain, by the end of which I was a lot wiser but no happier. I just couldn't come to terms with the whole concept of ponygirls, not really as a spectator and certainly not as a participant.

Not that I had any objections to nudity amongst likeminded adults. I was hooked on CP, found leather something of a turn on, especially the smell, and felt good about being fitter than I had ever been. But to wear a leather headdress, with a plume on the top making it even more absurd, a bit in my mouth attached to a set of reins, a small but tight corset nipping my waist in and knee-length boots, was taking it all a bit too far.

On top of all that, the ponygirl had to go between the shafts of one of the silly little carts and pull her driver wherever he or she wanted to go.

Then there was something about a tail, but by the time Jilly mentioned it I was already thinking it was time I wasn't there. In fact, if it hadn't been for Chrissie I am sure I would have left, but her bubbling enthusiasm kept me there, albeit on the fringes and not showing any interest.

But when Roger suggested that Jilly should put on her kit and show us what it was all about, I began to change my mind. As I have said, she was a striking girl and as Roger and Chrissie gradually transformed her from a fit young lady into a ponygirl, she didn't look as bizarre as I had imagined she might. In her headdress, with its golden plume to match the natural colour of her hair, the tight corset which only covered her from below her breasts to her hips, and her tight boots, she was definitely worth a second look. She stood in the middle of the barn, proud and erect, not in the least self-conscious and, as I followed Chrissie and Roger as they walked round her to savour her from every angle, I thought she was really rather stunning. I couldn't see that I would enjoy being dressed like that, but I did enjoy looking at her.

I saw how the boots enhanced the length and shapeliness of her legs and how the corset made her terrific breasts look even bigger and firmer. I stopped behind her and looked at her bottom. Again, the corset seemed to make it look different, but definitely without lessening the effects of its good points, mainly her excitingly tight cleft and sharply defined folds where cheek met thigh.

Then I moved round to her front and looked into her face, expecting to see some sign that she wanted my approval, but she gave nothing away, which threw me.

Her lovely blue eyes stared into the distance. There was no resentment in her expression, but neither was there much else. She looked at ease, but with a paradoxical, barely discernible restlessness about her. And it began to make a little sense.

My distant memories of that Irish farm became a little clearer – especially of the horses. They had often acted similarly when they were saddled and ready to be ridden, rattling their hooves on the courtyard stones, sweeping their tails around and gazing into the distance. Jilly was entering into the role.

And Roger added to the illusion. He paced around her, talking softly, stroking her cheek, telling her she was a beautiful girl. He ran his hands up and down her legs and squeezed her buttocks, then brushed her plume and adjusted it so that hung correctly. He dabbed a smear of petroleum jelly on the corners of her mouth and then pressed the bit in. She worked it around inside her mouth until it was comfortable and, as he clipped the reins to the ends, began to toss her head, eager for the off. Her plume waved elegantly above her.

Chrissie and I took one of the carts and pulled it out of the barn into the courtyard, and I was amazed at how light it was, and impressed with the quality of the construction. I remembered how much Greg's skill and ingenuity had added to the pleasure of our pillory, and it began to dawn on me that if Roger and Jilly were prepared to put the same care and effort behind making the wherewithal for their hobby, there just had to be more to it than met my eye.

We went back inside and I saw that Jilly was much more restless and couldn't keep her eyes off Roger as he moved to the rack of tails. He found one, raised it to the light so that the dark gold hair – matching her plume perfectly – shimmered exotically. Jilly made a little whinnying sound and stamped her feet; clearly the tail had some special significance, apart from completing her transformation.

'Down,' Roger ordered, but Jilly just tossed her head and stamped her feet, her bare bottom quivering as she did, and everything was beginning to get much more interesting.

'Down,' he repeated, and gave her a sharp slap on the hip, inducing another whinny, but she went down, first onto her knees, then forward, thrusting her hips up and back. I was standing right behind her and had a lovely view of the changing shape of her bottom as she presented it. I could clearly see her sex between her thighs, the moist pouting lips clearly visible through her soft downy hair, and distinctly kissable.

It was a mouth-watering sight to say the least, and although I still didn't understand exactly what was happening, my own sex began to tingle with anticipation.

Then I forgot about all that when Roger inserted her tail. Again, the ingenuity behind the design impressed me, even though I didn't get a chance to look at it in detail until later. But I could see that the hair was connected to a shaped plug, which narrowed smoothly near the join and which was obviously meant to nestle securely in the pony's rectum. It was about five inches long and thick enough to make a girl with a virgin bottom think at least twice about the wisdom of having it inside her.

Jilly's bottom was obviously not virginal, as the plug slid in quite easily and the operation was fascinating to watch. Because of the way the plug widened in the middle, I could clearly see the stretching of her sphincter muscle as that bit went in, and then closing round the narrow neck.

Once inserted she rose gracefully to let Roger fix an almost invisible cord to a hook on the lower hem of her corset. He adjusted it, and then stood back to let Chrissie and I have a good look. It really was a bizarre sight. The actual base of the tail rested tightly against her skin a little above the summit of her cleft, and was so clever it looked for the world as if it was really a part of her. It also had a pronounced outward curve so that, when seeing her from the side, it arched well clear of her buttocks.

I walked slowly around her again, shaking my head in disbelief, and again noticed that she was in no way put out by the way she was being displayed. If I had sensed the slightest reluctance on her part I would certainly have left. I may not have known her that well but I had grown fond of her, and would have hated to see her humiliated against her will.

We were then shown how the well-trained ponygirl struts her stuff. Jilly trotted out to the cart, which we had positioned with the shafts on the ground, not up in the air, and knelt between them, again lifting her bottom. She took hold of the handles at the ends of each shaft, Roger strapped her hands to them, picked up the reins, sat carefully in the padded seat, settled down and shook the reins so that they slapped against her shoulders.

'Hup!' he called, and she got up, leaned against the handles, tossing her head and shifting her hips so that plume and tail shimmered. 'Walk on.'

I saw the muscles in her thighs tense as she took the strain, but once she got going it looked relatively easy and she trotted up and down the courtyard, with Roger's touch on the reins light and sympathetic.

It wasn't long before I was quite enjoying myself. Coming towards us, Jilly made a great sight; her firm breasts bobbing and her toned thighs quivering.

The brief glimpses of her side and rear were tantalising; just a flickering impression of golden naked flesh and a twisting cleft under her swaying tail as she cantered past. Then most of her was hidden by Roger and the cart, leaving only her head and plume visible.

Eventually Roger brought her to a halt in front of us and she stood there, breathing deeply but steadily, her breasts heaving and shiny with sweat, her thighs flexing. In that relatively short time she had moved from bizarre to outlandishly beautiful.

Chrissie was vibrating with excitement and fired all sorts of technical questions at Roger while Jilly mouthed her bit and shook her head. I just drank in the sight of her terrific body and hoped Roger would drive her round again. He didn't, but after a while I no longer minded. He climbed off the cart, told Jilly to get down, unstrapped her hands, unclipped the reins and then took her bit out. She licked her lips and made an odd snuffling noise. He grinned at her as he stroked her face, then slapped her bottom and disappeared into the barn, appearing soon afterwards with a sugar lump, which he fed her from the palm of his hand. She nuzzled the lump with her lips and crunched it with relish and then bent forward to see if he had another. He didn't and she received another slap, so I sidled round to look at her bottom and was delighted to see that both cheeks had lovely pink blotches on the meatiest part. The slaps hadn't sounded that hard, but obviously his timing was spot on and I looked at him with greater respect, wondering how I could get him to spank me some time.

Jilly then had her gear taken off, with Chrissie demanding to be allowed to extract the tail, which she did with great pleasure and with my help – well, somebody had to hold Jilly's buttocks apart so she could see what she was doing. They were lovely and smooth and warm, by the way.

We were both intrigued by the intricacy of the mechanics of the tail. At the end of the plug there was a flesh coloured and flexible strip of plastic, which was so thin it was almost invisible when in place. The tail itself was fixed to this and, where they joined, a length of clear fishing line went up to the hem of the corset and held it all in place.

Roger explained that each of the regular ponygirls had her own tail, literally made to measure and with nylon threads selected to match the colour of her own hair.

'Why don't you use horse hair?' Chrissie asked.

'Too heavy,' Roger replied.

Jilly was then rubbed down with a damp cloth, dried and given a drink of water. After that she was back to being herself, and turned to Chrissie and me with an anxious look on her face. 'What did you think?' she asked.

'Fantastic!' Chrissie beamed, then everyone turned to look at me. I thought for several moments, trying to reconcile the various contrasting elements. I kept thinking about the tail and especially the plug, as I had last seen it before Roger took it away to sterilise it. I remembered the row of whips, and it was easy to imagine that they would usually be used to correct a stupid or stubborn pony. I wondered what it would feel like, my head enclosed in leather, a tight corset, a thick plug filling my rectum, a handsome tail which would occasionally brush nicely across my bare buttocks, and supportive boots.

Whoever drove me would have a lovely view of my bottom and, as long as it wasn't too vicious, I wouldn't mind at all if they whipped it every so often.

Another thought occurred to me; Roger and Jilly had worked brilliantly together. There was this instinctive communication between them that was much more than simply practised manoeuvres round the yard. It made me appreciate that it was very much the same between Chrissie, Susan, Jonquil and me, but with spanking rather than driving. With all three of them there was the sense of working to the same end; two minds, one arm and one bottom, all directed to a combination of correction, sensual pleasure and deep satisfaction for all concerned.

My instinctive resistance was ebbing away, but I still felt unable to commit myself as enthusiastically as Chrissie had done. However, on the other hand there was the thought that for all my reservations about Morganna and her torture chamber, I had been there twice and knew deep down that I would go again.

'Tell me more,' I eventually said, and both Roger and Jilly looked relieved, and immediately a stream of information burst about my ears.

I gathered that they had regular meetings, with all four carts in use. That there were two main challenges; dressage, where the ponies and riders dressed up in their full regalia and performed complex manoeuvres in the yard; and simple races, one against one.

It was already sounding far more interesting.

Then Jilly clinched it. 'The best bit – well almost the best bit – is the way losers pay their penalties. The winning pony gets to spank the loser. On her bare bottom, of course, and with everyone watching. Then the winning rider whips the losing pony. Not viciously but hard enough to stripe her bottom nicely. Sometimes the riders will have a side bet between themselves and the loser has to pay a penalty. That can be highly entertaining.'

I cursed myself for being too naïve to realise that there was bound to be more to it than simply prancing around, and looked at their faces, managing to suppress the grin of relief which threatened to break out.

'Concept sold to the redhead with the bare bum,' I said to grins all round, and first Roger and then Jilly gave me a nice hug and an affectionate kiss, followed by Chrissie, who declared that although she could hug and kiss me every day, she still didn't see why she should miss out. Suddenly I felt incredibly randy, and even more so when Chrissie suggested that my indecisiveness deserved a sound spanking. Naturally I protested my innocence and said it wasn't fair, and Roger and Jilly agreed that I had been quite right to give the matter serious thought before committing myself – but then added that I should be spanked anyway.

'What for?' I wailed, but the jury was unmoved, my fate was sealed and we cleared away and locked up before setting off back to the house.

In the sitting room an appropriate chair was positioned and I obediently lowered myself across Roger's knee, immediately feeling something hard pressing into my left hip. After my poor bottom had been suitably dealt with – and I soon learned that Roger really was a very good spanker indeed – Chrissie and I were measured for our accessories. As Roger explained, to get the tail to hang properly it was vital to have an accurate measurement of the distance between anus and top of the cleft. To find this we stood upright, the beginning of the valley between our buttocks was marked with a felt-tip, then we had to kneel down and lift our bottoms and a pair of geometry compasses used. To my relief, the point used to mark the centre of the anus had been safely embedded in a cork. Both Roger and Jilly had to agree that they had measured us properly, so that it took rather longer than strictly necessary, not that either Chrissie or I had any objections.

Roger very diffidently asked if we could contribute to the cost of the equipment and I gave him a cheque there and then, feeling that considering the amount of work and skill involved, the amount was reasonable to say the least.

It would take about four weeks before our equipment was ready, and Roger promised to arrange a full meeting of their pony society, as he called it, in five weeks' time to introduce us.

'And break you both in,' Jilly added, with a rather ominous glint in her eye.

Unfortunately, things were a little quiet on the agency front during that period, so as we had few distractions my reservations about the whole pony scene returned. In retrospect, what really concerned me was the probability of looking completely foolish. Chrissie was naturally far more athletic than I would ever be and would make a great ponygirl, so for some bizarre reason

I actively looked for excuses to punish her. So much so that her buttocks were almost permanently coloured, and we both began to realise that when the big day arrived she would show everybody a marked bottom.

So I thought up other ways of dealing with her, and the thought of the tail plug provided one little inspiration. When I found fault with her I would tell her to bare her bottom for inspection, and if her buttocks looked sore I would order her to kneel and lift it for me, exposing her anus. I would keep her like that for several minutes while I gloated over the extremely rude display, then kneel behind her and slap both her holes; obviously only hard enough to sting a little bit, but having to keep her bottom absolutely still made it into quite a testing little punishment.

As a finale I would then insert something into her bottom. If I was only mildly annoyed, it would merely be one finger, but I would always make her lick the selected digit first, adding to her humiliation. I would thrust it deep until my knuckles were cushioned against the flesh of her buttocks, and wriggle it around until she was gasping. Stage two was a couple of fingers, and the ultimate was a vibrator. For that she had to lubricate her own bottom – something I always thoroughly enjoyed watching.

Mind you, it was not all one-way traffic. My bottom came in for its fair share of attention and it all helped keep the doubts and uncertainties at bay. We had our regular enemas and enjoyed them as much as ever. However often I saw Chrissie's bottom in every little detail, I still got a big kick from following up the stairs to the bedroom, the tray with the jug of hot soapy water, lubricant and the enema itself proving a tricky enough load to make her walk up carefully. My eyes would be glued to her bare bottom as it rounded, dimpled and slowly swayed. I would focus on her cleft, excited at the prospect of seeing it slowly widen as she knelt for me, exposing that pretty little hole, which I would then toy with, so that by the time I was ready to apply the jelly she was shuddering with lust. I really loved slipping a finger into her rectum, feeling the clinging warmth.

Then after she expelled the water there was the regular pleasure of helping her in the shower, washing every inch of flawless flesh and always ending up by holding the adjusted flow up against her sex, watching the streams of water flowing over her bush as she finally orgasmed.

Then it was her turn to attend to me, and being done was just as delicious as doing.

With two weeks still to go before our initiation, I really did feel that it was getting on top of me. Clive and Jonquil came down for the weekend and we all had a great time. I spanked Jonquil again and she let Clive screw me. With her and Chrissie urging him on, I wrapped my legs round him, gripped his straining buttocks as hard as I could and rode with him to a great climax. He was even bigger than Roger or Greg, and when he asked me to take it in my mouth before he fucked me, I was afraid he would inadvertently choke me. But I loved it. Not that it came anywhere near replacing the much more involved pleasures of cunnilingus, especially with

Chrissie. Apart from the fact that I really did love her, her sex tasted delicious and the sight of her glistening, juicy clitoris as the immediate target for my tongue, was much more exciting then even the most handsome cock. But I did enjoy the change, very much.

We didn't mention the pony society to them. Roger and Jilly had sworn us to secrecy – for very obvious reasons – and we couldn't be sure whether Clive and Jonquil knew about it.

The calming effects of their visit lasted several days and Chrissie and I reverted to long walks and exploratory drives, our normal social contacts at the local, and gentle lovemaking.

We also talked a lot about future videos and spent many happy hours running through action sequences with each other, perfecting camera angles and discussing plots which would be both realistic and entertaining.

We agreed that the pillory could be used again, and wrote a couple of treatments for it. The first was a similar scenario to the finale of *Nightmare*, with a couple of young women in vaguely Victorian costume, newly appointed wardresses in an institute for the correction of errant females, being shown how to fasten a girl to the pillory, to make up a birch and then to apply it, firstly on their bottoms and, once they had the hang of it, punishing a prisoner for real.

In complete contrast, we plotted another film showing CP as a sexual thing, with a male and female couple trying out a number of implements, purely for their mutual enjoyment.

Clive had mentioned that the *College Tails* videos were selling very well, and we agreed there was little harm in repeating the same basic plot that we'd used in the first one, with Susan punishing a couple of girls and then agreeing to let them do the same to her.

Eventually our things were ready and, both excited and nervous, we dashed over to Roger and Jilly's house to try them on. I have never been wildly keen on clothes and shopping for them, but I was very keen to see how that lot fitted and felt.

An hour later we were standing in the courtyard, all dressed up, two carts ready for us and my heart thumping away like mad. It was definitely a new and different experience and I was having difficulty deciding how I felt about it.

The most obviously unfamiliar feeling was having the tight corset squeezing my middle uncomfortably. The headdress was much easier to wear than the leather mask Morganna had forced on me, and the smell of leather was familiar and sensual. The bit, a strip of tightly plaited leather, was surprisingly comfy and again, I liked the smell and taste.

And my tail felt great. The narrow neck of the plug meant that my sphincter was hardly stretched at all, and yet the plug itself was thick enough to fill my rectum beautifully. It was all very secure, and overall I didn't feel as uneasy as I'd expected.

I had expected Chrissie to be much more graceful and correct than I was, and my fears were confirmed from the beginning. I found it pretty hard to get balanced and co-ordinated, with the corset making bending difficult, the cart with Jilly driving heavy, especially to get it moving and the unnatural leg actions demanded of us awkward. But Jilly and Roger were patient and helpful, and by the time I panted to a halt for the first time I was a bit more confident. And the swim after our first training session was sheer bliss, although the spanking that both our hosts administered – just for the sake of it – was hard, long and painful.

We drove back home in silence. As far as I was concerned, my worst fears had not been realised but I still felt I would rather stick to straight CP, perhaps with the occasional bondage session, especially if Morganna was in charge.

Chapter Eight

At last the day of reckoning came. Chrissie and I were the first to arrive, and after we had undressed and been escorted to the barn, my doubts hit me with a vengeance. All the carts were lined up, shafts to the ground, each with a long thin whip balanced on the seat.

The dressage area had been sanded, and in the paddock beyond the barn straw bales marked out the course for the races. To my intense relief we were not going to compete in the dressage, as we were far too inexperienced to do ourselves justice. We had to watch instead, which suited me down to the ground.

Jilly helped us on with our corsets and headdresses, but when I began to bend over to have my tail put in, she told me that everyone watched that operation, which made me feel even less enthusiastic. But again I realised I was not being logical, after all, I had presented my naked bottom to be spanked in public often enough.

Then Chrissie had an inspired thought. 'This could make a great video,' she whispered. 'Give it some thought as we go,' and her idea made all the difference to me, as did the general atmosphere around the place.

Soon four other naked girls turned up, greeted us with real warmth and then two men and two women followed them, all in smart riding gear, with top hats, black coats, stocks and britches. They made us both very welcome and made it clear that we had all the time in the world to learn.

With Chrissie's suggestion in my mind, I began to see a possible film – the ponies arriving, getting undressed and walking to the barn. Then the drivers also getting changed; men and women mingling together, totally at ease.

We six ponies were then led to the paddock and left there while the drivers had coffee. The four experienced girls grew quieter, speaking less and nuzzling together, acting more and more like real ponies, really getting into their roles and clearly enjoying it.

My eyes flitted around my companions, mentally composing interesting shots, not just to show their bodies in a sexual contest, but also their latent athleticism as they stretched their legs and trotted around to warm up their muscles. I did the same, and despite the corset and headdress the sense of freedom was wonderful. Or was it, I wondered, because of the corset? Did the contrast between restricted waist and naked breasts and buttocks make the latter feel better than when I was completely naked?

Eventually we were called, and scampered back to the barn, where we were each taken by one of the drivers and had our bits and reins attached. Then it was time for the tails, and the air of excitement was intense. I was last, Chrissie next to last, so we could watch the others kneel down and present their bottoms. Again, I could so easily imagine how I would make a really exciting sequence of it.

With tails in place, Roger decreed that all six ponies

would parade round the yard on leading reins, showing off their paces. I began to see that there was real beauty in it all. Plumes and tails swayed and shimmered in the sunshine, and naked flesh glowed healthily as we warmed up in the fragrant fresh air. Lovely firm breasts bounced and quivered, and nipples puckered and hardened almost immediately. Naked buttocks swayed. Sculptured thigh and calf tendons became more defined. Clenched white teeth gleamed, bared by the efforts of their owners. Boots pounded rhythmically and threw little clouds of dry sand into the still air.

When it was my turn I soon understood why the other girls' nipples had reacted so blatantly. With all eyes watching me I found it a very enjoyable exercise.

The downside was that I was horribly aware of my clumsiness in comparison with the others; even Chrissie had managed to trot and cavort reasonably like a proud pony, whereas I took what seemed like ages to find any sort of rhythm, and wasn't in the least surprised that my driver gave my bottom several sharp flicks with his whip. Because of my tail he couldn't hit me across the full width, but had to aim for the side of the left buttock. They stung quite sharply, but not as much as the length and threatening appearance of the whip had suggested, so that there was one less thing to be worried about.

Eventually I was brought to a halt, led by the bridle part of my headdress back to the other girls in the paddock, given a drink of water, a rubdown with a deliciously cool damp cloth, and a piece of raw carrot. As I crunched it I realised that most of the other ponies had been given sugar lumps, and wondered why I had been treated differently. Was it a sign that I was out of favour? Then I remembered that Jilly had reminisced about having lumps of sugar as a treat when she was a girl, and I'd pulled a face. Later she mentioned raw carrot as a nice nibble and I agreed with her that it was one of my favourites, so I was again impressed with their attention to detail.

Chrissie and I stood by the paddock rail watching the dressage equally carefully, but with different agendas. She was doing her best to memorise as many of the complex moves as she could, while I had my film director's head on and was seeing it mainly as a spectacle and, slowly but surely, as an exotically exciting one.

The four ponies had been harnessed to the carts, each in turn kneeling with arms stretched out to the handles and bottoms up in the air, had been trotted round the yard to warm up, and then gone through the intricate movements demanded by the two judges, Jilly and one of the men who followed the competitors around, making frequent notes and consulting earnestly after each round.

Even I began to see a pattern emerging after a while, and although I was not at all confident in my ability to do much more than plod around reasonably accurately, the thought of eventually being allowed to join in was no longer daunting. All the ponies were touched up with the whip, even though I couldn't see that they had done anything wrong, and I visualised my bottom ending up a mass of weals!

The last outfit trotted back, the pony was unharnessed and the drivers tended to their charges while the judges conferred. I could sense a new tension in the atmosphere and Chrissie and I huddled close together, waiting expectantly on events.

I looked around, breathing deeply. I still had the bit in my mouth, so the taste and smell of leather were with me all the time, but not so dominant that I couldn't appreciate the warm air of late summer, the occasional waft of sweet, warm, scented girl flesh from one of the ponies, the hint of creosote and paint from the fences and outbuildings..

The last pony was groomed and refreshed and the four drivers led their charges back into the yard and stood in a line waiting for the judges' verdicts. I heard Jilly's voice going through the results, but didn't really listen. I was too captivated by the scene; the riders in their neat jackets, hats and britches in startling contrast to the lovely ponies.

Then movement in front of me interrupted my reflective thoughts; each pony had her tail removed, their corsets and headdresses were taken off, and they carried them into the barn and then got back into line out in the yard, again with their backs to us. I then noticed a significant difference in the girls' body language. By getting rid of the accessories they were no longer acting like ponies. They were back to being girls, naked except for their boots and with no sense of shame. They ran their fingers through their hair, rubbed the marks on their bottoms, flexed their thighs and stretched their backs and shoulders.

They did look a little anxious, and not surprisingly, as I was about to discover. I hadn't noticed that the two male drivers had disappeared until they came back into view, carrying a thick post. I frowned, wondering what was going on. Together they slotted the post into a hole in the ground, tested it to make sure it was firmly positioned, and went back to the barn. In a couple of minutes they emerged again with a sort of padded beam on legs, which they put down a couple of feet from the pole; I still couldn't work out what was going on.

'It's a whipping post,' Chrissie whispered, and it was as though a hand had gripped my insides and squeezed, consternation and a sheer sexual thrill vying for prominence.

The results of the competition were announced and three of the girls immediately showed signs of nervous tension. The one on the right, a lovely leggy brunette, noticeably relaxed, so it was quite obvious that she was the winner. My focus wandered from her to the others, and was more than happy with the selection on view.

My worry was that all the preparations suggested quite a severe punishment, and I was not really in the mood to see these apparently very nice girls in any pain.

Then the girl on the left of the line, the one who'd come last, I supposed, pulled back her shoulders and walked purposefully up to the waiting apparatus, rested her front against it and stretched her arms up towards the top. Roger quickly tied her wrists to a ring there, eased her feet apart and strapped them to the supporting legs of the beam, and then rejoined the other drivers.

The scene was set and my mouth watered at the prospect of capturing something very similar on camera.

In the background by the paddock fence were Chrissie and I in full ponygirl regalia. In front and slightly to our left were the drivers, still looking immaculate. To our right the three naked girls, two of them seemingly under some stress, shifting from foot to foot.

And last but not least, the centre of everyone's attention, the lovely loser. I thought how I would place and move the camera, panning slowly in from full length to a close-up of just her bottom. Even from some metres away I could see that it not only looked gorgeous but was very nicely posed for her whipping; curving out enough to make it pronounced and accessible, but keeping the flesh of her buttocks plump and soft so that the whip would sink in beautifully. I lusted over the mental image of me editing the sequence and repeating the first lash in slow motion, then in series of freeze-frames, pausing on the last few, showing the whip actually hitting her and the flesh swelling out on either side of the line of impact.

The vision was mouth-watering but the reality was just as good, even if it did lack that sort of detail. The loser got six strokes, the third placed girl four and the runner-up two.

Each left a bright red line right across their bottoms and each one seemed to cause no more pain than strictly necessary to ensure that it was worth trying to win. None of the girls cried out in pain or protested; they bravely tossed their heads, stamped their feet, clenched then shook their afflicted buttocks. There was the occasional whispered 'Ahhhh...' but nothing more.

After each punishment the chastised girl walked steadily back into line, and if their cheeks were flushed and their expressions strained, there were no visible tears.

It was, in fact, almost a perfect demonstration of CP for fun rather than punishment. On the bare bottom, hard enough to present a real challenge to the submissive recipient, to give the active one a real test of his ability and to give the spectators something really worth watching.

As far as I was concerned, only a sound spanking would have matched it for entertainment. For one thing, it would have lasted a lot longer and I felt then as I do now, that the sight of a girl draped gracefully over someone's knee, her buttocks naked and wobbling as the measured slaps slowly redden her soft flesh takes, if you'll excuse the pun, a hell of a lot of beating.

For the finale the winner walked to the post, did not have her hands tied, and the other three approached in turn, kissed both cheeks of her bottom all over, parted them and buried their faces in her cleft, presumably under orders to lick her bottom-hole, which encouraged me even more; it was reassuring to know that we weren't the only ones to enjoy that deliciously sluttish caress.

Two hours later my wish had been granted. After the awards ceremony, Chrissie and I had our accessories removed and I discovered that having the tail plug eased out was even nicer than having it inserted, we were washed, groomed and then told to join the other girls in the paddock, where we were fed. I thought we were going to be returned fully to normal, but I was yet again wrong. We may have had our harness taken off but I soon gathered that talking was out, and apart from that our food was served in large enamel bowls, placed on the ground so that we had to go on all fours to eat.

It felt peculiar to start with, but I was starving and the others all got stuck in without hesitation, so it was head down bottom up and to hell with any thoughts about dignity. The mixture of chopped apples, carrots, nuts and cereals was delicious, and the water in the small trough we drank from was cold and pure.

After we'd eaten we played at being ponies again. With the drivers back in the house we had the freedom of the paddock, and made full use of it. Fed, watered, soothed and rested, it seemed logical to do what ponies do in similar circumstances and chased each other around the paddock until we were blown, stopping to nuzzle somebody until we had our breath back and then starting again.

It sounds a bit silly and childish, but it was as enjoyable a half hour as I can remember. I loved being naked in the fresh air, and all the girls were very attractive and hadn't the slightest hesitation in enjoying looking and touching, or having their bodies admired. Therefore I was somewhat sorry when the group of drivers returned and whistled us to the gate.

Then it was back to being ponygirls again. We were fitted with everything except our tails, and Chrissie and I were led to a pair of carts. I stepped between the shafts, knelt down, lifted my bottom, had my hands tied and then stood up on command.

'We are going to test our new ponies with a little race,' Roger announced. My heart rate rocketed and I began to tune mind and body for intense physical effort. I glanced quickly over to Chrissie and saw her pert breasts rise and fall as she filled her lungs. Her plume waved as she stretched her neck and she looked so gorgeous I wanted to bed her there and then. But I couldn't, and so I concentrated on the race.

We each trotted round for a little to warm up and I quickly worked out that we were not expected to be graceful; speed was of the essence.

We lined up at the start and I dug my toes in. I could hear and feel my heartbeat and had the inspired thought that if I ever did make such a video, I would have the soundtrack consisting of nothing but the hollow throb of the pony's heart, getting faster and faster as the flag was raised. I was just deciding that I could also use the same gimmick when a girl was waiting for the first spank or stroke, when the starter dropped his flag and my left peripheral vision was filled with a rapidly accelerating Chrissie.

Cursing under my breath I drove off hard with my thighs and pushed against the shafts at the same time. I heard a faint whistle, then a fleshy crack and a line of pain exploded across both my pumping buttocks as Jilly spurred me into action…

I tried my utmost, but was not surprised to lose. Not only did I have that poor start to overcome, but Chrissie had been an excellent athlete at school and college, so she knew how to pace herself. I did catch up with her at one point, but made my move too soon and fell back well before the finish. But I didn't really mind, because according to tradition I had to be spanked by Chrissie and then whipped by Roger. I was more than happy to submit to the first part, and my curiosity about the effects

215

of the second virtually overcame my reservations.

Chrissie admitted afterwards that she had been too tired to do my bottom justice, but even so, it was a pretty good spanking and for once I was really glad to have an appreciative audience. Only the drivers were allowed to speak of course, and they were kind enough to make sure that I could hear their complimentary comments on the shape and consistency of my buttocks, and how well I was taking it, and what a lovely red bottom I ended up with.

The whipping was obviously far more testing. Walking up to the post, my bottom stinging, and knowing that all eyes were glued to my blotchy flesh was pretty awful, and the hollow feeling in my tummy when I meekly offered up my hands to be tied to the whipping post brought back some of those conflicting feelings which had disturbed me when Jonquil first spanked me.

With my experience on both sides of the camera, I could also work to make it an even better spectacle, and at the same time appreciate the sweet and sour pleasures of it all, from the feeling of utter helplessness after I'd been tied, to the subtle and sexy prominence the position gave my bottom.

I saw Roger from the corner of my eye, shifting his feet as he gauged his distance. I then closed my eyes and held my breath.

It did sting – a lot more than the flicks I'd taken in harness but not as much as Morganna's efforts. After each stroke I tossed my head and churned my hips, but it was as much for effect than from necessity. I was in a strange state, through a combination of excitement, physical tiredness, sensual and sexual stimulation and increasing pain. Part of my mind reminded me how much it adds to the occasion when the whipped girl's bottom writhes, then stills and gets pushed out in silent invitation for another, and I was very keen to give the watching group as much excitement as I could. Another part was simply rising to the challenge of the mounting pain and finding that actually concentrating on the movements of my bottom made the sensations even sharper.

The sixth and last stroke did make me cry out and really churn my bottom around, but the sting faded quite quickly and, while Roger was untying me, I was beginning to enjoy a terrific afterglow, both mental and physical.

That concluded the entertainment, and the drivers signalled the return of equality by helping us put everything away and lock up. Then it was back to the house and straight into the refreshing pool, where there was a lot of disgracefully rowdy ducking, diving, pushing in and helping out, all of which I enjoyed to the full. But after a while I drifted down to the deep end, floated on my back and just relaxed completely.

I was pretty weary, but above all I was incredibly happy that all my silly fears and doubts about ponygirls had been completely unfounded. It had been a wonderful day and I fully intended to have a quiet word with Roger about making a video as soon as possible.

I wondered if ponies ever took a turn at driving, and the prospect of inserting a tail into another girl's bottom really appealed – although I would have to practice to use one of those whips; on Chrissie's adorable buttocks, naturally.

My mind drifted pleasantly, lingering on some of the images left by our extraordinary day. The line of ponygirls waiting to be whipped had been very sexy, and I just had to incorporate something similar in a spanking video.

And gradually the ideas formed. I'd set it in the near future, when all the PC drivel had been seen to be pathetic and erring women were publicly chastised for breaking the law. I'd use at least four of them, stripped from the waist down in a waiting room... having to walk anxiously to the punishment room... sitting on a cold wooden bench, with their buttocks protruding over the edge. They would have to be spanked first, of course, to warm them up. I couldn't direct a CP film with no spanking at all. Then, perhaps, I'd choreograph a sensual paddling before the cane. Yes, and to finish, a lecture from the sadistic governor in charge, warning them what would happen if they offended again. Showing them the whips and birches that would be used on their bottoms. They'd be a row of lovely but penitent and subdued girls, seen from behind, their naked bottoms red and marked, trembling and tensing as whips are cracked in the air. Oh yes, I liked it.

But in the meantime there were those four lovely ponygirls to get to know better... a lot better.

So I flipped over onto my front and swam lazily back to join them in the shallow end.

More exciting titles available from Chimera

Sales and Distribution in the USA and Canada:

LPC Group
1436 West Randolph Street
Chicago
IL 60607
(800) 626-4330

* * *